To plant a garden is to believe in tomorrow.

—AUDREY HEPBURN

Savannah Secrets

The Hidden Gate
A Fallen Petal
Double Trouble
Whispering Bells
Where Time Stood Still
The Weight of Years
Willful Transgressions
Season's Meetings
Southern Fried Secrets
The Greatest of These
Patterns of Deception
The Waving Girl
Beneath a Dragon Moon
Garden Variety Crimes

Savannah Secrets

Garden Variety Crimes

BETH ADAMS

Danbury, Connecticut

Chapter One

JULIA FOLEY LOOKED UP FROM the stack of papers on her desk. She didn't know how long she'd been hunched over these files of phone records, but her shoulders were tight and her neck was starting to hurt. She sat back in her office chair and stretched her arms up. Background check cases might pay the bills, but they could be tedious. Her eyes were going bleary. She needed a break. She pushed herself up from her desk and walked out into the hallway. The smell of coffee filled the space. Meredith must have recently made a fresh pot. She walked over to the doorway of Meredith's office and poked her head in.

"I'm going for a walk," Julia said. "Want to come?"

"It sounds nice, but I've got to finish writing up this report today, before the kids come." Meredith took a sip from the steaming mug in front of her. Meredith's grandchildren, Kaden and Kinsley, would be spending a week of their summer vacation with Meredith, and Julia knew Meredith had been looking forward to it for weeks. "Need a break, huh?"

"Being a private investigator always looks so glamorous on TV. They never show the parts where you're studying documents for hours on end."

"I suppose that wouldn't make for very good television," Meredith said.

"I guess you're right." Julia sighed. "All right. I'm headed to the park. Give me a call if you need me."

"I'll be here trying to find a nice way to say this employee is definitely committing insurance fraud."

"So much glamour," Julia said. She headed down the hallway toward the front of the old Victorian that served as the headquarters for Magnolia Investigations. She waved at Carmen Lopez, who looked up from her screen at the front desk. "I'm going out for a bit."

"Enjoy the sunshine."

"Thank you." Julia braced herself for the wave of humidity she knew was coming, and then she stepped out onto the front porch. It wasn't too bad today, actually. It was still hot, naturally, but that was normal for early June in Savannah. Julia crossed the street and took in a deep breath as she stepped into Forsyth Park.

Savannah was known for the parks and squares, dotted with fountains and flowers and dripping with Spanish moss, that punctuated the historic district. Forsyth Park was the most famous. It was also one of the largest, stretching for six city blocks and filled with gardens and playgrounds and walkways and hundreds of nooks and crannies to explore. Julia felt lucky that she got to work right across the street from such a charming oasis, and today, as most days, she felt the tension drain from her body as she stepped under the canopy of live oak and palmetto and magnolia trees.

She turned down a narrow path that led away from the main lane that would take her to the park's famous fountain. The main walkways were clogged with tourists, selfie sticks at the ready, but Julia enjoyed the cool shade of the less populated areas of the park. She took in several deep breaths and let them out slowly. And then, just as she was starting to feel her shoulders unhitch, her cell phone rang, and she reached into her purse to dig it out.

Cassie, the screen said. Julia's younger sister. The tension came right back.

"Hi there," Julia said.

"Hi, Julia. How are you?"

"I'm all right. Enjoying the sunshine at Forsyth Park."

"That sounds nice." Julia waited for Cassie to say why she was calling. She didn't call just to chat. Cassie had moved back to Savannah earlier this year after decades of living out west trying to "find herself" and rarely touching base. "What's going on?"

"I wanted to let you know about a 5K Madison and Kennedy's school is doing to raise money for a new air conditioner for the cafeteria. It's on its last legs, and they're hoping to replace it before the kids come back in the fall. The race is in three weeks, and Wyatt is going to run it, and so am I. I wondered if you wanted to run it too."

"A 5K?" Julia was definitely not a runner, and if Cassie was, that was news to Julia. But that wasn't what had really thrown her off. How had Cassie heard about this fundraiser before Julia had?

"A 5K is just a little over three miles."

Julia stopped in the shade of a crepe myrtle and considered this. Madison and Kennedy were technically Cassie's grandchildren, though Julia usually considered them her own, as Cassie had been out of the picture for so much of their lives. How had Cassie known about this? Still, if their school needed new air-conditioning, Julia was glad to help. But a 5K?

"I would love to help, of course," Julia said. "But how about I just make a donation? Where should I send the check?"

"I mean, I'm sure the school would appreciate the check, but I was hoping this would be something we could do together. As sisters."

As sisters? Cassie said that as if they often did things together as sisters.

"I haven't run in years, Cassie," Julia said. "Decades. I'm not sure I could run three miles if a bear was chasing me. I think I'd rather end up as bear food."

"That's why you'd train for it," Cassie said. "You don't have to be able to do it today. But if you start training now, you could do it in three weeks."

"I don't know." Was there a polite way to say she'd rather cut off her arm than run a race in Georgia in June? What were they thinking, scheduling a 5K for this time of year? "Are they having a bake sale at any point? I'd be better at that. I make a mean strawberry rhubarb crisp."

"They might have a bake sale. I don't know. But I do know they're having this race, and I know it would mean a lot to the girls if you could do it." After a pause, she added, "It would mean a lot to me too."

Julia hesitated. In all honesty, the last thing she wanted to do was say yes. Running was terrible. And she couldn't deny that a small, petty part of her was annoyed that Cassie had learned about the fundraiser before Julia had. But still. Cassie had said over and over since she had come home that she wanted to be a part of their lives, and now here was evidence. Julia didn't know how she could say no, no matter how much she wanted to.

"You can walk part of it if you need to," Cassie said. "Or I'll help you get to the point where you can run."

"All right." Julia let out a breath. "I'll do it."

"Awesome. I'm so glad. This is going to be fun."

Julia very much doubted that. She actually thought it was more likely that Cassie would bail out on her just before the race and leave her to do it on her own. But Cassie had said she wanted to do this as sisters. If Cassie was trying, then Julia could try too.

"I'll bring the entry form by tomorrow. And there are all kinds of training plans online, if you need help building up to three miles."

"That sounds great."

"Awesome. Gotta go. See you!" And with that, Cassie hung up. Julia stood still for a moment, trying to process what had just happened. Had she really just gotten talked into running a 5K with her flaky sister in the heat of summer? She shook her head. She supposed it would make her empathize with the need for air-conditioning at the school.

She tucked her phone back into her purse and started walking again. She meandered through the pathways and side lanes of Forsyth Park and soon found herself in a section in the northwest corner of the park, standing in front of a row of azaleas in full bloom behind an iron fence. Julia smelled the flowers, and then a flash of light behind the plants caught her eye. Was something moving back there?

Julia leaned forward and tried to see through the bushes, pushing branches out of the way, but the foliage was too thick. She couldn't see anything but shadows, but then—another flash. Something behind the bushes had caught the sun.

Julia looked around. As far as she could tell, the whole area was set off behind the waist-high iron gate. It was pretty clear you weren't supposed to go back there. And yet—

She craned her neck to the right, and then back to the left. Someone—or something—was back there. Julia wanted to know why.

There was no one coming from either direction. Somehow, in this crowded park, this quiet corner way off the main path was secluded. Julia walked down the path and found a slightly wider opening between two azaleas. It wasn't much, really little more than a space with fewer branches in the way, but Julia thought that if she—

She looked around one more time, hiked her leg up over the iron fence, pushing the branches out of the way as best she could, and then hopped over the fence.

"Oof." Well, that hadn't been graceful, but she'd made it. Leaves brushed against her face, and she spat out an azalea petal. When she pushed through the bushes, she found herself in a small enclosed area between the hedges and the fence, and it was…

It was magical. Live oaks draped with moss sheltered a garden of the most stunning flowers Julia had ever seen. Big soft petals were white on the inside and a deep purple on the outside, and they looped and gathered around a base that looked like an old-fashioned trumpet. Stunning smaller purple flowers—were they a kind of bluebell?—grew along delicate, slender stalks. Bell-shaped blooms in gorgeous shades of pink grew next to heads of little white blossoms and a plant with small eggplant-colored flowers and glossy blackish-purple berries.

Julia leaned in closer to the first bloom that had caught her eye. The petals were arranged in such an intricate and unexpected manner, and the petals' purple outside made the colors blend and swirl like no flower she'd ever seen. It was stunning. Julia felt as though she'd stumbled into a magical little garden planted just for her.

She straightened up and looked around. No one was here, and whatever had caught the light was gone too. Could she have imagined that? She thought a moment and then realized it wasn't possible. She had seen something earlier—something that wasn't visible now. Had someone been back here, looking out for this magical little fairy garden?

But why was it planted so far from where someone could see it? Why weren't these flowers on public display? Everyone should be able to enjoy stunning blooms like these.

Julia looked back again at the purple and white swirl. It was incredible. But what was it?

Julia thought for a moment and then remembered an app she'd downloaded onto her phone when she'd been planning out the annuals she wanted for her yard this year. She'd seen small pink flowers in the tree beds beneath the magnolias along Whitaker Street and been desperate to know what they were so she could plant them in her own yard. Carmen had recommended the app, which could analyze a photo of a flower and suggest what it probably was. Julia didn't understand how it worked, but she did know that it had correctly identified the Sweet William and also led her to a local garden center where she could purchase the variety.

Julia took her phone out now and held it out, trying to get a good angle for her shot. She lined it up, took several photos, and uploaded them to the app. She hit the button that said FIND IT! and waited while the app analyzed the photograph. Then it returned the name of a flower Julia had never heard of: DATURA.

Datura? Julia read the text that followed: A GENUS OF NINE SPECIES OF POISONOUS VESPERTINE FLOWERING PLANTS BELONGING TO

THE FAMILY SOLANACEAE. ALSO COMMONLY KNOWN AS JIMSON WEED, MOONFLOWER, AND DEVIL'S TRUMPET.

Poisonous? Julia took a quick step back, eyed the flower, and then looked down at her screen and back up at the beautiful bloom. Could this really be the same flower? It was so astonishingly beautiful—could it really be poisonous?

INGESTING DATURA CAN LEAD TO HALLUCINATIONS, TACHY-CARDIA, GASTROINTESTINAL DISTRESS, AND DEATH.

What in the world? The app had to have gotten this wrong. What would a poisonous plant be doing in a public park? But when Julia used her phone to google datura, the images that came back looked exactly like the flower in front of her. Could this stunning flower really be deadly?

Julia looked around again. No one else was there; this magical little garden was well hidden. Could it be here by accident? Maybe someone had planted this flower without knowing what it was? Or—was it possible someone had put it here on purpose?

But why?

It couldn't be allowed to stay here, that was for sure. Someone could pick such beautiful blooms and take them home and… Well, Julia had to tell someone these were here before anyone got hurt. Julia walked back to the azaleas and pushed her way through the branches again. She clambered over the fence, and then she made her way back to the main path. She didn't know where to find whoever was in charge, but there had to be someone. She found herself walking along the main central path that led to the fountain, and after a little way, she caught sight of a man in the short-sleeved green uniform shirt of the parks department employees. He was using a broom and an industrial dustpan to sweep up a popsicle wrapper.

"Excuse me," Julia said when she got close. "I'd like to talk to someone about a plant in the park."

The man stared back at her vacantly. "What plant?"

"It's off in the northwest corner of the park, behind the azaleas. It's datura. It's poisonous."

Again, the man simply stared, his expression blank.

"Do you know who I would talk to?" Julia asked.

"I'll call Randy." The man reached to the walkie-talkie on his waist and said, "Randy, this is Evan from facilities. There's a lady here who wants to talk about a poisonous plant."

Julia couldn't make out Randy's response over the garbled line, but Evan nodded and indicated a bench nearby. "He'll be here in a few minutes," he said. He went back to sweeping up garbage, and a few minutes later, another man in a green polo shirt appeared and conferred with Evan, who gestured to Julia. Julia stepped forward and walked up to the man.

"Hi. I'm Julia Folcy," she said.

"Randy Torrez. Director of Greenscapes for Forsyth Park," the man said. He looked to be almost her age, and his belly strained the fabric of his shirt. "Evan said something about a poisonous plant?"

Julia nodded. "I think it's datura."

His eyes widened. "Here? In the park?"

"I could be wrong," Julia said. "I'm not a gardening expert or anything. But my app told me that's what it was, and I wondered why it was here in a public park."

"That is a very good question indeed," Randy said. "If you're right about it being datura, there's no way that should be here. It's highly toxic. Where is it?"

"In that lovely hidden garden behind the azaleas," Julia said. "Near the corner of Gaston and Whitaker."

"Hidden garden?" Randy was staring at her like she was speaking a foreign language.

"Yes, that beautiful little secret garden…" But as she spoke, she started to understand how silly the words sounded.

"Why don't you show me where this is?" Randy suggested. Julia nodded, and as they walked, she told him what had happened—how she had been walking through the quiet section of the park and had seen a flash of light and had climbed over the fence and through the bushes—

"You hopped the fence?" Randy eyed her. She wasn't sure if he was doubting her ability to climb fences or whether he was gently rebuking her for breaking the rules.

"I thought someone was back there," Julia said, and then, when his expression didn't change, she added, "I'm a private investigator."

Randy nodded, as if this explained it all, and Julia decided not to belabor it anymore.

"I climbed back through here," Julia said as they arrived at the gap in the azaleas she had gone through. She climbed back over the fence once again, and then she pushed her way through the bushes, and soon they were standing in front of the hidden garden once again.

"Holy moly," Randy said slowly, taking in the blooms arranged before them. "What in the world?" He stepped forward and leaned in and looked more closely at the plant with the deep purple berries.

"So this is not supposed to be here?" Julia asked.

"No." He laughed. "No, this is very much not supposed to be here."

"Is it datura, then?" Julia felt strangely proud to have spotted the plant before he had.

"It's datura, all right." Randy let out a sigh. "Unmistakable. And this?" He pointed to the berries, so dark purple they were almost black. "Do you know what this is?"

"No idea."

"That plant is called atropa belladonna," Randy said. "Otherwise known as deadly nightshade."

"I'm—" Julia took a small step back. "What?"

Randy nodded. "And that right there"—he pointed at the flowers she thought might be bluebells—"those are monkshood."

"Monkshood?"

"The flowers are said to look like monk's cowls," Randy explained. "It's poisonous too. And if I'm not mistaken, it looks like we've got foxglove, hemlock, and angel's-trumpet here also."

"Are they all—"

"Highly toxic." He nodded.

"Why is there a hidden garden filled with poisonous plants right in the middle of Forsyth Park?" Julia asked.

Randy stared at the flowers, his eyes wide. "I sure would like to know that myself."

Chapter Two

Dearest Eugenia,

How are you finding Charleston? What is your new home like? Is it right on the water, like Owen promised? Are there interesting people? Are you enjoying yourself? I do so hope that you are settling into your new home.

No, wait, that is not true at all. I hope you hate it and come back soon, because things are dreadfully dull here in Savannah without you. There is no one interesting to talk with at the parties these days.

To wit, it seems that Martha Billiot has recovered from her illness. Some found it rather remarkable that her stomach problem struck just before June Winslow's garden tea, but I told them all that she did not hold June's slight against her, and that we all know Martha could not have attended her party because of her family obligations even if she had been invited. Still, without you, and with Martha "indisposed," it was the most dreadfully boring party of the season.

Janine Hatcher came visiting today, and she was full of the most interesting news. It seems that India and Fred Dixon are selling their place on Abercorn. Rumor has it that Fred lost all his money investing in that shipping scheme he was telling everyone about last winter. Do you remember how proud India was of the fireplace tiles she had shipped all the way from Amsterdam? It seems some other family will now get to enjoy those hand-painted tiles. It's such a shame. We must pray for them.

I heard today that Daisy has refused to give up her little project. She should never have been allowed to travel overseas. Foreign climates spoil the mind, if you ask me. She has those girls jumping around indelicately and has the temerity to say it's good for them. How she can think it's good to rattle their insides like that, I'll never understand. I think Daisy really has crossed the line now, and I don't know how Nellie can hold her head up.

Melanie Dale's garden is looking quite beautiful this year. The roses are in full bloom. You would love it. I don't know how much it cost to have those lovely pink varieties imported from England, but it was worth every penny.

Write back soon. I am bored beyond belief.

> *Yours,*
>
> *Hattie*

The air-conditioning felt lovely as Julia stepped inside the office. She took in a deep breath and let the door fall softly closed behind her.

"How was your walk?" Carmen looked up from the open filing cabinet drawer.

"It was…" Julia didn't know how to respond. "Not what I expected."

Carmen's brow wrinkled. "How so?"

Julia let out a sigh. "Well, I discovered a magical hidden garden and then discovered it was filled with plants that can kill you."

"What?"

"I showed it to a park ranger, and he—"

"Hold up." Meredith was already walking down the hallway toward them. She must have overheard and was now coming to hear more. "What was that about plants that can kill you?"

"I found a garden, hidden over a fence and behind some azalea bushes, over by Drayton Street," Julia said.

"What were you doing over a fence and behind azalea bushes?" Meredith asked.

Julia explained how she had seen movement and the flash of light and discovered the garden and identified the plant as datura. "And then when I brought a ranger over to see, he identified several other kinds of poisonous flowers," she continued.

"Why was there a garden of poisonous plants in Forsyth Park?" Carmen had pushed back from the filing cabinet and was looking up at Julia.

"I don't know. They don't know who planted it or why."

"So it was not supposed to be there," Meredith said.

"No." Julia fluttered the hem of her shirt to move the cool air around. "The ranger said they were going to have them ripped out as soon as possible, but I just hope no one else discovers the plants in the meantime. What if someone picked a flower, not knowing what it was? It could kill them."

"Did the ranger call the police?" Carmen asked.

Julia nodded. "He said he was going to. I don't know that a crime has been committed, but it can't hurt to have something like this on record, in case someone does get hurt, or...worse."

"Now that's a morbid thought," Meredith said.

Julia nodded. But she'd been a judge in the Georgia court system long enough to understand how important it could be to leave a paper trail.

She saw that Meredith was pressing her lips together. "What is it?"

"I was just thinking about something I heard," Meredith said. "I don't know if it's related. But..." She held up one finger and then walked quickly back to her office.

Julia looked at Carmen, who shrugged. "No idea," Carmen said.

A moment later, Meredith came hurrying back down the hallway and into the reception area again, holding a newspaper. "I saw this article this morning," she said, setting the newspaper down on Carmen's desk. Carmen quickly scooted her keyboard out of the way. Julia saw that it was the local section of the *Savannah Morning News* before Meredith flipped it open and started paging through it.

"There was an article about how several dogs recently got sick after visits to Forsyth Park," Meredith said. She found the page she was looking for. "I noticed it because when I was at the diner last week, Rhonda told me her dog had been sick and she was wondering if something he'd eaten in the park had caused it." She pointed at the article in the paper. "It says here other animals have been reported sick after visits to the park. I wondered if it was related."

Julia looked down at the paper and read the headline: *Dogs Reported Ill after Walks in Forsyth Park; Owners Searching for Answers.* The garden was behind a fence, and dogs weren't supposed to be off their leashes in the park. Could a dog have gotten back there? Julia didn't see how this could be related. "Does it say where in the park the dogs were?"

"No, it doesn't," Meredith said.

"Are those flowers toxic to dogs as well as people?" Carmen asked.

"I imagine they would be," Julia said. "If they can kill a person, surely they can kill a dog."

"I wonder if they're connected," Meredith said. "That would be so terrible, if someone knowingly planted poisonous flowers and they caused dogs to get sick."

"Wow." Carmen shook her head. "I hope they get those plants taken out right away, before any more dogs get sick." And then, a moment later, she added, "Or people."

"And I hope they find out who planted them," Meredith said.

Julia didn't say anything for a moment. Randy, the parks department guy, had said he would have the police look into it. But surely that didn't mean she had to just sit back and wait.

Carmen started to laugh. "I know that look. I think I know who's going to find the culprit. You're not going to leave this to the police, are you?"

"I thought I might do some asking around," Julia admitted. She and Meredith had solved a number of mysteries in the year since they had opened Magnolia Investigations. Why not see what she could find out about this? "It can't hurt to have more people looking into the matter, can it?"

"You really don't want to work on that background check, do you?" Meredith asked with a smile on her face.

"You're right," Julia said. "I really don't. But I also want to see if I can help figure out who made those dogs sick and stop them before another one gets sick, or worse."

"What are you going to do?" Meredith asked. Her head was cocked; she was intrigued, Julia could see.

"I was thinking I might pay a visit to my friend Jan Lynch."

"I met Jan at your Christmas party," Meredith said. "The gardener. Strong cheekbones, Gucci glasses, big cushion-cut diamond."

"That's right," Julia said. Meredith did have an eye for details. That's what made her good at what she did. "She's a friend from church. She's very involved in the Garden Club of Savannah, and she knows many of the people who garden around here."

Meredith nodded. "That's a good idea. Whoever planted those flowers obviously knows a lot about gardening. She might have some ideas."

"That's what I was thinking," Julia said. She could call first, but Jan loved visitors. If she was home, she would be thrilled to see Julia. "Would you be interested in coming along?"

"As much fun as that sounds, I need to finish up this report so I can get home before the kids get here," Meredith said. "But let me know what you find out."

"I will." Julia waved at Meredith and Carmen, and then she headed back out into the summer heat.

Jan lived in a historic home just off Oglethorpe Square. It would be quicker to walk, Julia decided, and she set off, dodging tourists and locals out for a stroll. She found the large brick home with black shutters easily enough. Julia climbed up the wooden steps to the wide porch and rang the doorbell. It echoed inside, then the door opened, and Jan cried out, "Julia!" She was wearing a floor-length sleeveless dress in a bright floral pattern. "How are you? Come in."

"Hi, Jan." Julia hesitated. "Are you on your way out?"

"Oh no, I'm just reading." She stepped aside to let Julia enter. "I'd love a visitor."

Julia didn't usually sit around in dresses as nice as that one, but that was Jan.

"It's so lovely out. Let's sit in the garden," Jan said. Julia followed Jan as she led her through the formal parlor. Jan's house had been featured in last year's homes tour, so Julia knew that the walls of this room, painted with faded but beautifully detailed frescoes of nature scenes, had been imported from a castle in France. The celestial scene on the ceiling had been commissioned to complete the room and had taken master craftsmen three years to finish. They walked from the parlor into a smaller living room and then into a chef's kitchen with high-end appliances and marble counters. A woman in a dark uniform was slicing an onion at the counter and didn't look up as they passed through and stepped out into a lush walled garden.

"This is stunning," Julia said as Jan led her down the steps and into an urban paradise. Camelias, climbing roses, gladiolas, and lilies were in full bloom, and creeping jasmine and hyacinth gave off a sweet scent. Honeysuckle and morning glory vines twirled around a pergola, creating a shady oasis where a table and chairs were set, along with a two wicker rocking chairs. A fountain burbled softly in the corner.

"Thank you," Jan said, indicating she should sit in one of the wicker rocking chairs. "We spend as much time as the weather will allow out here."

Julia sat down, and Jan sat next to her. Julia noticed a late-model cell phone and a paperback book, spine up, on the small glass-topped table between the two chairs. It was miraculously cool under the trellis, and it took Julia a moment to discover the misters spraying tiny droplets of water into the space.

"So," Jan said, "how is everything? How is Beau? Alex was talking to him at church last week and told me he's looking into downsizing his boat?"

Julia shrugged. Now that her husband was retired, he spent most of his free time fishing, and he was always talking about new gear of some kind.

"I'll believe it when I see it," she said, shaking her head.

They chatted about Jan's recent vacation to Brazil and Julia's favorite new avocado salad recipe and the new type of rosebush Jan was having brought in from Italy for the corner of the garden. At some point, the woman from the kitchen brought out a pitcher of sweet tea, and Jan thanked her and poured them both a tall, icy glass. Then the topic finally turned to the reason for Julia's visit.

"I was walking in Forsyth Park this afternoon," Julia said, "and I came across some strange plants." She told Jan how she had identified the purple and white flowers as datura, and how she had brought over a ranger who told her all the flowers in the garden were poisonous.

"There was belladonna? And monkshood?" Jan's eyes were wide.

"That's right," Julia said. "All planted together. They made the most beautiful garden—the datura flowers were just stunning—but then I found out what they were, and I grew worried that someone might accidentally get hurt, or worse."

"Well, yes, they could," Jan agreed, nodding. "I do hope the authorities get those plants removed right away."

"The parks department said they would," Julia said. "And they also said they'll be looking into who planted them, but then I got to wondering…"

Jan laughed. "Because that's what you do." She took a sip of her tea and held the glass for a moment, letting the ice cubes tinkle gently against the side. "I don't know much about poisonous plants. I took a class at the Savannah Botanical Gardens once, years ago, where they talked about how dangerous many of those plants are and cautioned us against accidentally including them in our gardens, but that's really the only way I know of them."

Julia hoped she wasn't detecting a note of defensiveness in her friend's tone. "I was actually wondering, because you're so well connected with many of the gardeners in town, if you knew of anyone who might know anything more about the plants."

"I'm sure none of my friends knows anything about those particular plants," Jan said.

"Of course not," Julia quickly added. "Naturally I don't think anyone you know planted those flowers in the park. I was just hoping to talk to someone who might be able to tell me where you can even buy plants like these."

"Right." Jan nodded. "That makes sense." She set her glass down gently. The diamond on her left hand caught the sunlight, casting brilliant prisms around. "I do know most of the best gardeners in town."

"Exactly," Julia said. "That's what I was thinking too."

"Well," Jan said, "in that case, yes, I imagine I know some people who might be able to tell you a bit more about this sort of thing."

"I'd be most grateful," Julia said, relieved that Jan wasn't offended with her questions.

"I'd start with Larry White," Jan said. "He's the one who taught the class at the Botanical Gardens. He's the head gardener there and knows more about plants than anyone I've ever met."

Julia nodded, feeling silly. She should have thought of checking into the Botanical Gardens for more information herself. But now she had a name, which would help.

"Go ahead and give him a call and say I recommended you speak with him. I'm sure he'll be glad to talk to you."

Jan sat back in her chair, slouching into the thick cushion.

"Let's see. Who else? Mary Catherine Nunez knows a lot about exotic plants," Jan said. "I don't know if this is up her alley at all, but she might be worth talking to. She may know someone. Oh, but you know what? She's in Europe for the summer. That won't help. But Elyse Cheney might be worth talking to. She was in that class I took at the Botanical Garden. She seemed…" She let her voice trail off for a moment. "Well, she seemed to know a strange amount about the toxic plants," she finally said. "She kept talking about hemlock, like she was a character in a Victorian novel."

"Interesting. Do you have any idea why she knew so much about hemlock?" Julia asked.

"I didn't ask, though maybe I should have," Jan said. "I said that if her husband turned up dead, we'd know why, and she laughed. But as far as I know, he's strong and healthy, so there's no reason to worry."

"I'm glad to hear that," Julia said. She noted the name. Knowing about or being interested in poisonous plants was not the same as poisoning someone, but Elyse was probably worth talking to.

"I'd have to dig up her contact information," Jan said. "I think she was on an email chain I was on."

"I would appreciate it."

Jan picked up her phone. "I can't think of anyone else who would know anything," she said. "But I'll put you in touch with the ones I mentioned."

"This is a wonderful start," Julia said. "I really appreciate it."

Jan gave Julia the contact information, and Julia entered their numbers into her phone. "I'm anxious to hear what you find out," Jan said. "Whoever planted those flowers—they have to be stopped, obviously."

"I couldn't agree more." Julia nodded. "And I thank you for the leads."

They chatted for a while longer, and then when Julia excused herself and said she would let Jan get back to her day, Jan graciously showed her out.

As Julia walked back to the office, she called Larry White, the director of the Savannah Botanical Gardens. She got his voice mail and left a message for him, saying she was a friend of Jan's and asking if she could talk to him about some unusual flowers.

The temperature had dropped a few degrees as the sun slipped lower in the sky, but Julia still walked in the shade as much as possible. She had just turned onto Whitaker Street when her phone rang. It was a local number but one she didn't recognize.

"This is Julia," she said into the phone.

"Hi, Julia. This is Larry White, returning your call."

"Thank you so much for calling back," Julia said. "As I mentioned, Jan Lynch gave me your name—"

"If you're a friend of Jan's, you're a friend of mine," Larry said. "I'm going to be in my office for about another hour, and then I'm off the rest of the week, but I have a few things to finish up before I go. Is there any chance you're free to stop by for a bit in, say, thirty minutes? Then we could have a proper chat."

Julia looked at her watch. It was after four. It was only about a fifteen-minute drive, so she should have no trouble getting there in time. And if he was leaving for the rest of the week, this might be her only chance. She would have to call Beau to let him know she would be home a little late, but he could get the grill fired up.

"If you're sure you have the time, that would be wonderful."

"Great. I'll see you shortly."

***

Julia loved the Botanical Gardens. It was a magical place, from the rose garden to flower-surrounded fountain to the paths that threaded past the pond. Julia stopped in at the old Reinhard house, a nineteenth-century two-story farmhouse where the office was located. She made her way inside and found Larry White's office easily.

"Hello," she said, knocking on the door, which stood mostly open. A man she guessed to be in his fifties was staring at a computer screen, biting his bottom lip. He sat back when he saw her and took off his glasses.

"Hello there. You must be Jan's friend." He had a ring of gray hair around the crown of his head, but he was otherwise bald. The office was cramped, piled with books and papers on every imaginable surface, and it held the earthy scent of soil.

"That's right." Julia smiled. "Julia Foley."

"I'm glad you made it. You called at just the right time."

"You said you were going to be out for the rest of the week," Julia said. "Are you going somewhere fun?"

"My wife and I are headed to Greece for our twenty-fifth anniversary." He smiled, revealing a gap between his two front teeth.

"Congratulations. That's wonderful."

"Thank you. Francelle has been wanting to go there for a long time, and this year I ran out of excuses."

"I hope you have a wonderful time," Julia said. She had never been to Greece, though it had always sounded wonderful. Maybe she and Beau would make it there someday. "And I so appreciate you meeting me today, when you must be trying your best to get out the door."

"You have to admit, you gave me a pretty intriguing opening," Larry said. "You said you wanted to talk about some unusual flowers. And unusual flowers are pretty much my favorite thing to talk about."

Julia laughed. "It sounds like you're in the right job, then."

"Yes, I do enjoy it." He folded the stems of his glasses and set them down on the desk. "So what flowers did you have in mind?"

Julia told him about the discovery of the poisonous flowers in Forsyth Park, and his eyes widened. "Right there in the park?"

"That's right," Julia said. "They were tucked away in a corner behind some azaleas, so they weren't right out in the middle of everything, but still."

"And what varieties did you say were there?" Larry leaned forward, his wooden chair squealing underneath him.

"Datura, as well as belladonna—"

"Deadly nightshade." Larry shook his head. And then, seeming to realize that he'd interrupted her, gestured for her to go on.

"There was also hemlock, angel's-trumpet, and, I think, monkshood?"

"Goodness. All the highlights. Whoever planted them certainly was thorough."

"I suppose so. I'm hoping to find leads on who might have planted them."

"Of course." He unfolded his glasses and then folded them back again. "If it had just been one variety of poisonous plant, I would have said it was probably a fluke. You'd be surprised by how often toxic plants get planted in people's homes. My aunt in California had oleander planted all around her backyard because she liked the pink blossoms."

"Is oleander poisonous?" She'd seen the large plants with their colorful flowers all over Florida.

"Oh yes. Ingesting its leaves can kill you," Larry said. "A fact they found out after my young cousin decided to taste the leaves and ended up in the emergency room."

"But it's planted all over the place."

He shrugged. "Toxic plants are often planted unknowingly, and there's a surprising number of everyday plants that will make you sick. Hyacinth and daffodil bulbs, for one. Rhubarb. If you eat a large amount of the leaves, you can end up in a coma. Wisteria—hundreds of children are poisoned by wisteria seeds every year. Mistletoe berries can kill you. And of course cyanide is made from laurel, which you can find anywhere. People just like the way these plants look, and don't realize that the plants can do serious harm."

"Daffodils? Hyacinth? *Rhubarb*?" Surely she would have known if common plants like these were dangerous.

"Oh yes. Take daffodils. The flowers themselves won't do much worse than taste bad, but there are many recorded cases where someone was digging in the garden in early spring and mistook a daffodil bulb for an onion or head of garlic. The bulbs can mess you up in a big way."

"I had no idea."

"Most people don't know how many different kinds of plants can be deadly," Larry said.

As he spoke, she tried to decide whether he could know more than he was saying about the plants in the park. On the one hand, he did seem to know a lot about poisonous plants and seemed to love talking about them. On the other hand, he was so open and earnest and willing to share that it was hard to imagine he could be hiding anything.

"Do you think that's the case here?" Julia asked. "That someone planted the poisonous flowers by accident?"

"Oh no. Not in this case," Larry said. "While there are a lot of plants that will make you sick, the ones you mentioned are really the best of the best, if you're looking to kill someone."

Julia's stomach lurched, and he stopped as he seemed to realize how what he'd said could be taken.

"That's not to say that was the goal here," he said. "Just that, with all those species planted together in one garden, it's hard to dismiss it as a coincidence. It seems unlikely that those particular varieties would have been chosen by accident. And whoever planted them has to be someone who knows quite a bit about poisonous plants."

"I thought that as well," Julia said. "Do you know of anyone who fits the bill?"

"There's only one person who comes to mind," Larry said. "He's a professor over at Savannah State, in the biology department. He's on the board of the Botanical Gardens, and when we were chatting before our last board meeting, he mentioned a grad student who was working with some poisonous plants. I suppose you could talk to him and see if he could tell you any more."

"I'd be happy to." Julia knew Savannah State was the historically Black college in town, and it had an excellent reputation. "Do you have his contact information?"

Larry volunteered to put in a call to his friend Frank, and gave her his own contact information in case he didn't hear back from Frank before he left on his trip.

"Do you have any ideas how the flowers could have ended up in Forsyth Park?" Julia figured she might as well ask the question straight out.

"I don't," Larry said. "If you find out, I would sure love to know. I hope you find the answer. It would be a shame not to know who's behind plantings as unusual as that."

Julia left, not sure how to feel. She supposed the depth of his knowledge and the enthusiasm with which Larry had spoken of the poisonous plants should put him high up on her list of suspects. On the other hand, he just seemed so...earnest. Surely if he knew anything about the plantings in the park, he would have been more guarded, wouldn't he?

Julia didn't know what to think. She needed to learn more.

Chapter Three

TUESDAY MORNING, JULIA'S ALARM WENT off at six. She silenced it and crept quietly out of bed. Beau still slept, so she walked softly to the bathroom, where she'd set out her exercise clothes the night before. She slipped into her comfiest T-shirt and a pair of elastic-waist shorts and then went out to the porch and laced up her sneakers. It was already hot and muggy out, the sky a flat, steely gray. She stretched her legs on the porch and tried to loosen up as best she could, and then she walked down the steps. *Here goes nothing*, she thought.

She jogged lightly down the path before turning right and heading down the sidewalk. This wasn't so bad. By the time she got to the corner, her muscles had started to loosen up, and her arms pumped, and her legs fell into a rhythm. A very slow rhythm but a rhythm nonetheless. She had made it almost four blocks before she started to feel short of breath and her steps slowed, but she kept moving.

She turned at the end of the street and was now running down an avenue shaded by majestic elms and oaks. She had always loved the homes on this street, and she focused on admiring each one as she passed, trying to decide in her mind which she would most like to live in. It distracted her momentarily, but when she had passed that block, the pain in her lungs grew unbearable and she had to force herself to keep her legs moving. She couldn't even imagine what she must look like—a cross between a terrified giraffe and a wounded bear, she guessed. It was so unbearably hot.

She slowed her feet and began to walk. Slowly, with each step, her lungs hurt a little bit less, but now that her legs were moving more slowly, she felt the muscles cramp and ache.

This was awful. Why in the world would people run for fun? What was wrong with them?

Julia turned back in the direction of home and walked until her breath returned to a normal pattern. She supposed she should give it another try, maybe jog the last few blocks, but she couldn't make herself care enough to actually do it. She couldn't even make it to one mile. She definitely couldn't do the 5K. She would just tell Cassie that they would have to find something else to do together as sisters. She would write a check to the school and be done with it. This wasn't going to work. She quit.

***

Julia still felt flushed when she walked into the Magnolia Investigations office. She had stood in the shower, letting cool water rinse over her, until she felt better, but she found she was still sweating as she ate breakfast and got ready for the day. She had tried to tell Beau there was just no way she would ever be able to run a 5K, but Beau had laughed and, infuriatingly, suggested she simply needed to get back out there and try it again, promising it would get easier as she built up her cardiovascular fitness. The nerve.

"*¡Hola! ¿Cómo estás?*" Carmen asked as Julia came into the reception area. The air inside the office was cool, but Julia still went to the thermostat on the wall and cranked up the cold air.

"I tried to run this morning," Julia answered.

"Oh cool. I love the feeling after a run. No matter how much it hurts while I'm doing it, I'm always glad I went."

Julia cocked her head. What kind of nonsense was Carmen spouting?

"It's hard at first," Carmen said. "Just don't give up. It gets easier, and you'll eventually get to the point where it doesn't hurt as much and you start to like it."

"I don't believe you."

Carmen laughed. "Trust me on this one." Then she turned to her screen and said, "Meredith will be out today, right?"

"That's right. She's spending the day with her grandkids," Julia said. "So it should be quiet around here. I'll try to get that background check taken care of."

Carmen pressed her lips together, holding back a smile.

"All right, I also plan to spend some time seeing if I can learn anything more about those poisonous plants," Julia admitted.

"I knew it," Carmen said.

"I have a meeting later this morning with someone who supposedly knows a lot about hemlock." Julia had called Jan's friend Elyse, and Elyse had graciously invited Julia over at eleven.

"About what?"

"Hemlock. Haven't you ever read Agatha Christie?"

"Nope." Carmen shook her head. "Can't say I have."

"They're classics."

Carmen just gave her a funny look.

"Kids these days." Julia shook her head and walked down the hallway.

Carmen was hardly a kid. She was in her twenties and lived on her own, but Julia had met her when she'd shown up in Julia's courtroom as a child being shuttled from one foster home to another. Julia would probably never be able to see her and not remember the loudmouthed child she'd been, hiding her fear and pain behind an abrasive exterior. But despite her troubled past, Carmen had grown into a smart young woman and become an indispensable asset to the agency.

Julia heard Carmen laughing as she settled in her office chair. She turned on her computer, checked her email, and responded to the urgent messages. Then she turned to the manila folders stuffed with papers on her desk. She read through several credit reports, motor vehicle and driving records, and educational files, and then turned to her computer and opened up the service they used that checked for a person's criminal record. After verifying the applicant's fingerprints against the appropriate databases, she filled out the paperwork that declared Zara Beddoe passed the background check and Magnolia Investigations could find no reason why she shouldn't be hired as a substitute teacher for Savannah Public Schools.

Then she sat back and stretched her arms over her head. There were other cases she could start work on, but it was more of the same. Her mind was elsewhere—back in that hidden garden in Forsyth Park. She checked her email again and saw that Larry had sent her the contact information for Frank Elmore, the biology professor he knew at Savannah State University. She sent Professor Elmore a message, asking if he could spare a few moments to speak with her and leaving her cell phone number. She had that meeting later with Elyse, but—she checked the clock in the corner of her screen. She had time.

She pulled out her wallet, where she had tucked the business card Randy Torrez had given her, and she dialed his number.

"Hello?"

"Mr. Torrez? This is Julia Foley of Magnolia Investigations. We met yesterday, in the garden."

"Of course. How are you today, Mrs. Foley?"

"I'm doing well, thank you. It's just that, well, I haven't been able to stop wondering about those flowers."

"It was quite a strange thing to find," Randy said. "We've surrounded them with caution tape for now, at least until we can get them pulled."

"The plants haven't been removed yet?" Julia was surprised to hear that.

"We're waiting for the police to come take whatever samples they need. And then, of course, there are special precautions that must be taken when removing plants of this sort. We're researching the appropriate measures."

"I suppose that makes sense," Julia said. "I actually have a few more questions about those plants. Would you have any time today for a quick chat?"

"I'm free for the next hour, if you have a moment to come by. After that, it's meetings back-to-back."

"That would be wonderful. Where can I meet you?"

"I was about to head over to the fragrance garden," he said. "To check on some flowers we recently transplanted. Would you be able to meet me there?"

"That sounds lovely. I can be there in a few minutes."

"Give me ten, and I'll see you there."

"I look forward to it."

Julia pushed herself up, grabbed her purse, and headed down the hall. "I'm going to head over to Forsyth Park for a bit," she said. Carmen smiled and waved, and Julia stepped outside.

The morning's clouds had mostly melted off, leaving behind a hazy sort of sunshine, and the park was already filled with people. Julia easily found her way to the Garden of Fragrance, which was a special section of the park originally designed for people with limited sight. It was overflowing with fragrant flowers and interesting textures. The garden was surrounded by columns on three sides, but she found the wrought iron gates on the fourth side open, and she wandered through the rows of lilies, roses, irises, and rhododendron. The sweet smell was intoxicating. There were a few people wandering among the plants, but this section of the park was quiet.

"Hello there."

Julia turned and found Randy Torrez coming in through the gate. He wore the same short-sleeved green polo and khakis as he had yesterday, but he also wore a baseball cap to keep the sun off his face. He had a tool belt around his waist, filled with trowels and shears and hand rakes.

"Hi. Thanks so much for meeting me."

"Happy to." Randy gave her a grin. "How could I say no to the person who made the most interesting discovery in this park in ages?" As he spoke, he led her over to a garden bed planted with various types of lilies, ranging from pure white to vibrant orange and soft pink. The cloying scent was nearly overpowering, but he crouched down next to a bed of stunning pinkish-orange flowers.

"It was curious," Julia said. "I just hope no one gets hurt before the plants can be safely removed."

"We're doing everything we can," Randy said as he examined the blooms. "But until the police get in there to gather evidence, there's not much we can do."

"Did they say when they'll come?" Julia asked.

"Hopefully today." He shrugged. "Apparently they believe there are more important crimes happening in Savannah than some plants appearing in a garden."

"They won't say that if someone gets hurt," Julia said.

"I agree. I sure hope they make it today."

Julia nodded and then leaned in to get a better look at the flowers on the plant he was examining. "That's a beautiful flower. What type of lily is that?"

"It's called the matrix lily," Randy said. "We've been trying to get as many varieties of lily as we can in here, but the matrix has proven tricky. This one seems to be doing all right, though."

"It looks to be thriving."

He shrugged. "The problem is it could be thriving one day and dying the next. You just never know." He pushed himself up and moved over to a row of tender pink blooms. "Elodie lilies," he said, gesturing at the flowers.

"They're beautiful." Julia examined the double layer of soft pink petals. They truly were stunning, but she wanted to steer the conversation back toward the reason she had come. "Is your team responsible for all the plantings in the park?"

"That's right," he said. "I mean, we take no credit for that mess you found yesterday, but in general, yes."

"It must be a big job."

"Definitely a fun one, if you love plants."

"I guess that means you do."

He nodded. "Even as a kid, I was fascinated by them. The idea of coaxing something as gorgeous as this out of a tiny seed or ugly bulb? It will never stop amazing me."

It was beautiful, when he said it like that. Julia wished she knew more about plants. It would be nice to be the kind of person who nurtured and maintained a gorgeous garden.

"How many people are on your team?"

"There are half a dozen who work mainly at Forsyth Park."

"That many?"

"It's a big park." He shrugged. "And it's one of the most heavily trafficked of all the parks in the city."

Julia knew that to be true. Forsyth Park was one of the don't-miss destinations on every tourist itinerary, not to mention the locals who used it every day.

"Whoever planted those poisonous plants must have come to the park regularly," she said. "They weren't just planted there and left; they were well maintained."

"You're right about that." Randy straightened up and looked at her. "I think I see where you're going with this."

Julia waited.

"Can I ask what the nature of your investigation is?" He tilted his head. "You're a private investigator, right?"

"That's right," Julia said. "But my investigation is completely informal. I'm not working for anyone. Just curious and can't help myself."

He seemed to mull this over and then nodded. "The truth is, I wondered about this myself. Whoever tended those plants had to come here quite often, and somehow no one noticed them coming or going."

"The easiest way to avoid detection would be to look like you belong here," Julia said, finishing what he was suggesting. "A parks department uniform would mean no one would question your presence here."

"You want to know if anyone on this team was behind the plantings," Randy said.

Julia nodded, grateful she hadn't needed to say it out loud.

Randy looked around, as if checking to see if anyone was listening. The others in the garden were not within earshot.

"Look, I can't throw suspicion on any of my coworkers," Randy said. "But I can tell you that I had that thought."

Julia waited. Many people were uncomfortable with silence, and she'd found that sometimes the best way to get a person to say what you were hoping for was to keep quiet.

"The guy doesn't work in this park," Randy said. "So he's not actually on my team. He's new in the department, and he mostly works on mowing, trimming trees, that kind of thing—the stuff newbies have to do to put in their time."

"But you've seen him here in Forsyth Park?" Julia guessed.

"Several times," Randy said. "And every time, he's been kind of slinking around. Wearing the uniform, but with his hat pulled way down, sunglasses, as if he's hiding."

Julia had a thought. "If he goes from park to park, why wouldn't he work here sometimes?"

"Newbies don't work Forsyth Park." Randy shook his head. "This place is the crown jewel of Savannah. The guys who work here have been doing it for years."

"Huh." Julia thought for a moment. "Can you tell me his name?"

Again, Randy looked around. "Calvin Corliss," he said. Julia made a note of the name. "I'm not saying he's responsible, just that it strikes me as odd to see him around so much when he's supposed to be working elsewhere."

"It does seem strange," Julia agreed. "It's a good lead."

Randy brushed soil from his hands and checked his watch. Julia wasn't sure how much longer she had, so she asked another question she'd come to find out about. "I was wondering if there were security cameras in the park," she said.

"Oh sure," Randy said. "When they work, which is hit or miss. The problem is that even when they do work, they're focused on the places you would expect—the areas that are more highly trafficked. There aren't many located off the main paths, and none by where you found that hidden garden. I've already asked to have the footage pulled from the last few weeks. But I don't know how likely it is we'll see anything useful."

"Would it be possible to get a look at the footage when you get it?"

He shrugged. "I don't see why not. Maybe you'll see something we don't see."

"Thank you."

"I'll let you know when it's ready," Randy said. "Believe me, I want to find the person who did this even more than you do."

Julia realized it was probably true. As offended as she was by what she had found, Randy had to be even more so.

"Look, I'm afraid I have to get going if I'm going to make it to my meeting on time," Randy said.

"I appreciate your taking the time to talk with me," she said.

He pulled on the brim of his hat. "Anytime."

***

When Julia got back to the office, she planned to dive into research on Calvin Corliss, but there was an email from Frank Elmore waiting for her. The biology professor at Savannah State. Well, that was quick.

Ms. Foley,

I am intrigued by your question about poisonous plants. I don't know much about them myself, but I have a graduate student working in the lab this summer that I'd be happy to introduce you to. Poisonous plants are his specialty. Would you be interested in coming by to talk to him? Just let me know when would be convenient for you and I'll set it up.

Best,

Frank Elmore

Julia wrote back right away, asking if she could stop by this afternoon or tomorrow. An actual expert in poisonous plants! Now she was getting somewhere.

She scanned through the rest of her email and answered some queries about the agency's pricing and followed up on a few investigations in progress, and then it was time to head out to meet with Elyse Cheney.

She walked down the hallway and told Carmen where she was headed and then drove to Elyse's home, which turned out to be a palatial house on the Isle of Hope, with thick columns and a wide double porch. Julia knew that many of the homes in this area, about a half hour from downtown, had originally been built years ago as vacation homes for Savannah's wealthy hoping to escape the heat of the city. Elyse's home looked to be one of the original houses in the area, and the wide green lawn was framed by trees draped in Spanish moss. Julia pulled into the circular driveway and walked along the flagstone path bordered with blooming hydrangeas before stepping up to the door, which was covered by a white wood portico. She rang the doorbell.

"Hello. You must be Jan's friend."

Julia didn't know what she had been expecting, but she was surprised to find a young woman with blond hair that looked like it had a lot of help from a bottle, and a British accent.

"Hello. I'm Julia Foley."

"Mrs. Foley. It's nice to meet you. Please, come in." Elyse ushered Julia inside. It was nice and cool in here. Julia didn't even want to think about what it must cost to heat and cool this place. "Why don't we visit out on the porch? It's so pleasant out there this time of year."

She led Julia past a dining room with a polished mahogany table that had to seat at least twelve.

"Your home is lovely," Julia said.

"Thank you," Elyse said. "I like antiques, as you can tell."

"They're beautiful."

Elyse led her through a sunroom off the dining room and out onto the back porch. The porch stretched the length of the house and held several seating areas. Elyse led her to the one on the right, with two chairs and a loveseat made of wicker, with thick cushions in a muted floral pattern. The ceiling was painted haint blue, and ceiling fans stirred the air lazily. Julia sat down in one of the chairs, and Elyse sat in the other. A brown and white dog with a thick fur coat slept in the shade next to Elyse's chair.

"This is charming," Julia said. Over the porch rail, forsythia and laurel bloomed, and beautifully tended beds of petunias and asters flanked the sides of the yard. Past the sloping lawn, a long dock ran out into the Skidaway River, with a large boat anchored at the end. It was, probably quite literally, a million-dollar view.

"Thank you. I love to sit out here and watch the boats go past," Elyse said, nodding at a white-hulled fishing vessel that was chugging along the river.

"I can see why. This is lovely."

"I grew up by the seaside, and I missed it when we moved to Chicago, so when we moved here, I told Bryce we had to get a place by the water."

"Where did you grow up?" Julia asked. "I get the sense you're not from around here."

"Did the accent give it away?" Elyse laughed. "No, I'm not from Georgia. I grew up in a little fishing village in Cornwall. Not much to do but watch the boats go in and out. That's probably why I got into gardening. At least in a garden something is always changing."

"Your gardens are stunning."

"Eh." She waved the compliment aside. "It keeps me busy. Bryce works so much—he's in commercial real estate, and he travels all the time, so I need something to keep me occupied."

Julia thought about the huge house. She hadn't seen anyone else in it, and there was none of the usual detritus that indicated children lived there.

"I used to be a professional gardener, before I met Bryce," Elyse added.

"Oh really?" Julia tried to keep her voice level. "Where was that?"

"There's this lovely garden in Northumberland on the grounds of an old castle. It's very beautiful, and I loved it. But you know how it is. You meet the right one, and suddenly you're living in Illinois." She smiled. "It's been a change of pace being in the States, but the people here are friendly."

The dog sighed in his sleep, and Elyse reached down to pet him absently.

"So. Jan mentioned that you're a private investigator. That sounds like such an interesting line of work."

"It has its ups and downs, as most jobs do. But for the most part, I enjoy it."

"I'll bet you get to chase down all sorts of interesting cases."

"It's not as glamorous as all that," Julia said.

"Well, I can't wait to hear what flowers have to do with it. But hang on." She popped up. "I'll go get us some tea. I'll be right back."

She vanished inside the house, and Julia sat back and let her gaze rest on the river. A larger boat went past, carrying nets and poles. Julia decided it must be a commercial fishing vessel, and then, from the other direction, a small speedboat zoomed past, whipping a child on a tube behind it. Julia could get used to this.

When Elyse returned, she was carrying a tray, and Julia was surprised to see that she hadn't brought iced tea, the official beverage of the South, but hot tea, in a china teapot and hand-painted china teacups.

"I hope you don't mind the real thing. I can't abide the cold stuff." Elyse set the tray down on the glass-topped table. "I made Earl Grey. I hope that's okay."

"That sounds lovely."

As Elyse sat down, the dog at her feet stirred.

"Sorry, Charlie," she said.

"He's a pretty dog," Julia said.

"Thank you. He's a Shetland sheepdog. My family has always had shelties, but I feel bad for him having so much fur in this heat."

"I imagine shelties were bred for more temperate climates," Julia said. "He's beautiful, though."

Charlie stood up and walked over to a tennis ball that was resting by the side of the porch.

"Not now, Charlie," Elyse said. "The other thing about shelties is they love to run. He could play fetch for hours on end." She turned to the dog. "We'll play later."

"Well, don't let me stop you."

"It's hardly conducive to conversation." Elyse smiled. Then, as she poured the tea from the pot into the cups, she said, "So Jan told me you're interested in flowers, but she didn't say much more than that."

"That's right. I was walking in Forsyth Park yesterday when I made a strange discovery." Julia explained how she'd found the plants and learned what they were. As she spoke, something in Elyse's face changed. Julia couldn't read it, but if she had to guess, she would say it was fear she saw in Elyse's eyes.

"That's so strange," Elyse said. "Milk? Sugar?"

It was more than the look on her face or in her eyes. Elyse's whole manner changed when Julia mentioned the poisonous plants. Before, she had been open and talkative, but she seemed withdrawn now.

"A little of both, please," Julia answered.

"I'm wondering why Jan thought I might know something," Elyse said. "I'm afraid I don't often make it out to the historic district, and I almost never go to Forsyth Park." She kept her eyes focused on the tray as she added a spoonful of sugar and a splash of milk from a tiny china pitcher to Julia's cup and handed it to her.

"She mentioned that you had taken a class at the Botanical Gardens," Julia said. "And that there was some discussion of poisonous plants."

"Was there?" Elyse picked up her own teacup and sat back in her chair. "I don't remember that."

"She said the instructor warned against common poisonous plants and how to keep them out of everyday gardens."

"Huh." She shook her head. "I do remember that class. It was about the best perennials for this climate, and that's where I learned about false goatsbeard. I got that one"—she indicated a bush with a crown of bushy pink flowers—"after that class."

"False goatsbeard?"

"I forget what the formal name is. But isn't it beautiful?"

"It's stunning."

"But I'm afraid I don't remember any specific discussion about poisonous plants in that class."

Julia took a sip of her tea, trying to make sense of this. Had Jan been mistaken? She'd seemed so sure. And there was something in Elyse's manner that still didn't quite add up. Julia couldn't be sure—maybe it was just that famous British stiff upper lip—but she felt sure Elyse was hiding something.

"She mentioned something about hemlock...." Julia let her voice trail off. Jan had been quite sure that Elyse had spoken about hemlock, but now Elyse shook her head.

"I'm afraid I don't know anything about hemlock," she said. "It's one of those things you read about in old novels, isn't it?" She lifted the cup to her mouth and took a sip. There was a look of finality in it, and that's when Julia was sure she was lying.

"I assure you, I don't know a thing about poisonous plants," Elyse continued.

"I'm sorry to disturb you, in that case."

"Oh, I'm glad you did. Any friend of Jan's is a friend of mine. Now tell me, are you from this area yourself?"

She deftly changed the subject, and Julia told her about growing up in Savannah, working as a lawyer in Atlanta, and then being appointed as a judge in Chatham County's juvenile court. Elyse was friendly, but there remained something guarded about her that hadn't been there before.

Julia left feeling unsettled. She didn't believe Jan had been mistaken about Elyse's knowledge of hemlock. She was certain Elyse had been lying, but she had no way to prove it.

And not only that, she had no idea why.

Chapter Four

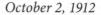

Dearest Eugenia,

The parties go on, even in your absence, but they are no fun without you. Caroline Wilkerson's coming-out ball really was dreadful. I didn't care for the food or the music (I believe that viola player was tone deaf) and I don't know why Ernestine thought that garish new hotel off Forsyth Park would be an appropriate venue. When did people stop building ballrooms in their own homes? It's the decline of civilization.

I'm sorry to hear about your trouble with your house-maid. Servants really are the bane of our existence, are they not? Why is it so difficult to find honest help? You'd think they'd be grateful for the opportunity to work in such a fine home. I believe the only way to get her to admit to taking your pearls is to withhold her payment until she returns them. If she still refuses, you are absolutely within your rights to fire her, but in that case you will never get your pearls back. You *have to have a firm hand. They will take advantage of every inch you give them.*

Did you hear what Daisy has her girls up to now? Marching around in uniforms like soldiers? It's shameful. No good will come of this, you mark my words.

Hattie

Julia picked up lunch at Hunter's, a local deli that made the best pastrami sandwiches, on the way back to the office. When she returned to her desk, she saw that she had an email from Frank Elmore, the biology professor, asking her to come by his lab at three thirty. He told her which building his lab was in, and Julia wrote back quickly to say that she would see him then.

She pulled her sandwich out of the paper bag, set it on the desk, and opened the waxy paper. She turned to her computer, opened up a search window, and typed in the name of the parks department employee Randy Torrez had mentioned: CALVIN CORLISS. Julia took a bite of her sandwich as she scanned the results.

She found a Facebook page with a profile picture that showed a burly man with shaggy brown hair and a mustache, and all he seemed to post were quotes he'd taken from other pages. His location was listed as Pooler, Georgia, a suburb of Savannah, so she was pretty sure she'd found the right guy. Julia ate her sandwich and read his posts as far back as the page went. Somehow, he'd avoided mentioning one personal thing about himself.

Julia cracked open the Diet Dr Pepper she'd bought with lunch and took the first satisfying sip. Fuel for the work ahead.

She went back to the search page and found a Calvin Corliss who was a track star at a high school in Texas, but that couldn't be him. She found a comment made by a Corliss on a discussion page about antiques, but she doubted that was him. Then, buried deep in the search results, she found a reference to a Calvin Corliss in the crime blotter section of the *Savannah Morning News* in 2015.

Police responded to reports of a two-car crash on Pine Barren Road in Pooler on Saturday at 11:30 p.m. They found a Nissan Sentra that had spun out and crashed into a Ford pickup. The driver of the Nissan, identified as Calvin Corliss of Pooler, failed a Breathalyzer and was arrested on charges of driving under the influence. The driver of the pickup was taken to the hospital and treated for injuries that were not considered life-threatening.

That was interesting. A drunk driving arrest didn't mean he was in any way connected to this case, but it did give Julia an idea. Court and arrest records were public data. She could find what happened when he was arrested and whether he'd been charged or whether he'd ever been in court for other reasons, but it was tedious work. Then she had another idea.

She stood and walked down the hallway. "Carmen?"

Carmen looked up from her computer.

"Do you have time for a little project?"

"Sure thing. What do you need?"

Julia explained the drunk driving arrest and said that she was interested in any arrest records related to Calvin Corliss. Carmen assured her she'd find whatever was there.

Julia thanked her and then walked back to her desk. It sure was quiet without Meredith around. She wished her friend was here to bounce a few ideas off of, but Julia knew she was spending time with her grandkids. It was good for all of them. Still, she was glad Meredith would be in for part of the day tomorrow.

Back at her desk, Julia took another sip of her Diet Dr Pepper and thought back on her visit to Elyse Cheney. She thought about that gorgeous house on the river that had somehow seemed so devoid of life. She knew Elyse was lying about the hemlock. Jan wouldn't have gotten that wrong, and Julia could see in Elyse's face that she was hiding something. The question was what, and why. She had to learn more. She decided to run a search on Elyse and see what turned up, but just then, her phone rang, and she saw it was Meredith. What was she doing calling on her day off?

"Hi there," Julia said. "How's it going with the kids?"

"Doorbell camera footage."

"What?"

"Kaden was showing me the view from the doorbell Carter and Sherri Lynn recently installed. You can see it on your phone."

"Hang on." Meredith sometimes got like this when she was excited, and it took a minute to get her to slow down enough so Julia could understand what she was trying to say. "You're talking about those doorbells that also have a security camera feature?"

Julia had seen them soar in popularity over the past few years. The doorbells came equipped with a camera that you could view from an app on your phone. It allowed you to see who was at your door before you answered it, and it also recorded footage, which was useful in case a package went missing, since the image of everyone who had been at your door was recorded.

"You're suggesting we look at doorbell cam footage, why?"

"These things are getting so common now. There have got to be houses and businesses around the park that have them. I'm thinking especially of locations near the section of the park where you found the poisonous plants."

Julia was starting to understand now. "You think that some-place that has a doorbell camera might have captured people going into the park."

"Right. If there's someone who shows up regularly in the footage coming into the park, that might be a person to investigate."

"Good thinking." Julia wished she'd thought of it herself. "I did ask about getting copies of the park's security footage, and they're supposed to give it to us when they have it, but this way we won't have to wait."

"And we'll get a different angle," Meredith said. "It's worth try-ing, in any case."

"You bet it is. Nice work."

"If you can't get to it today, maybe the kids and I can come in and help tomorrow."

"You don't need to—"

"Kinsley! Put that down!" And then, into the phone, "Gotta go."

God bless Meredith. Julia was glad she was getting to be with the kids. But it sounded like she had her hands full.

Julia checked the clock again. She didn't have enough time to go out and gather footage now. She had to head out soon to meet Pro-fessor Elmore at his lab. But it was definitely something they needed to look into.

***

Julia wandered around the Savannah State campus for a short time before she found the brick and glass building that housed the science labs. Once inside, she followed the signs to the second floor and pushed open the door marked ROOM 201—ELMORE. She didn't know what she'd expected to see—maybe serious scientists in safety goggles huddled over beakers—but what she found was an empty room that looked more like an office than anything. A desk sat in the center, and filing cabinets lined the walls. She closed the door behind her, and saw that hallways branched off to the right and the left. She waited for a minute, trying to decide how to announce herself. When no one appeared, she picked the left hallway and wandered down it and found a locked door. The black scanner pad next to it indicated you needed a key card to open it.

Julia was just turning back to the office to try the other hallway when the door opened and a young woman came barreling out, a black purse hung over her shoulder.

"Oh. Excuse me." She stopped and stepped back. "I didn't expect you there."

"I'm so sorry. I was looking for Professor Elmore."

"Oh sure. Dr. Elmore is back this way." She indicated behind her. "Do you want me to get him for you?"

"That would be great. Thank you."

"Hang on." The woman turned around and let the door fall shut behind her. Julia stood awkwardly in the hallway, unsure what to do, until the young woman returned, this time with a man near Julia's age behind her. He had close-cropped graying hair and chestnut-colored skin and wore a beautifully tailored suit beneath his open lab coat.

"Thank you, Antoinette," he said, and she nodded and smiled at Julia before continuing down the hallway and out of the lab. "You must be Julia Foley."

"It's wonderful to meet you," Julia said, reaching out her hand.

He smiled and shook it and then indicated that she should follow him. He led her into a large open room where half a dozen people sat at counters that lined the room, typing away on computers.

"This is a biology lab?" she asked.

Dr. Elmore laughed. "Not exactly what you picture, is it? Don't worry. There are plenty of the requisite microscopes and test tubes in the back. The sad truth is that biology experiments are dreadfully dull, because it takes time for life to, well, grow, so there's a lot of time spent waiting. These students are working on their data while they wait."

None of the students even looked up as he talked, and she realized most of them had earbuds in while they worked.

"Why are there so many students here during summer break?" Julia asked.

Professor Elmore chuckled. "Science does not take breaks." And then he added, "These students are mostly working on senior projects. It works out best for most of the science majors to stay on campus and get their research done over the summer, because it's much harder to fit in time-consuming research projects once classes and sports start up again."

"What sort of things are they researching?" Julia asked.

"We study plant biology here. My area of research involves studying the effects of altering plant DNA, and how that impacts generations down the line."

Julia nodded, vaguely understanding.

"So, for instance, I might look at corn that has been genetically engineered to resist a certain kind of insect. I study how that genetic mutation changes the structure of the plants grown from that generation of seed, but also the generations that come after that, and after that, and after that."

"That sounds really interesting."

"I think so." He smiled broadly. "All the students who are working here are helping me with that, but they're also all working on their individual senior projects focused on some element of plant biology."

"So they get to choose what they want to research?"

"Within reason." He shrugged. "It's always interesting to me to see what excites them. I have a student working on the impact of climate change on biodiversity in the seaweed found around our shores, and one who's studying whether crossbreeding irises can help make pollinators more efficient. And then, of course, there's Theo Williams, who is the student interested in poisonous and carnivorous plants."

"And he's here?"

"He's in the back. Follow me." He led her out of the open room and into a hallway lined with closed doors. He knocked on one toward the end, and a moment later it opened and a young man leaned out.

"Hi, Dr. E." Theo Williams wore a lab coat and had goggles pushed up on his head.

"Hello, Theo. This is Julia Foley. She's the one I told you about who's interested in poisonous plants."

"Hello, Mrs. Foley. It's nice to meet you." Theo stood and shook her hand. The hum of a ventilation system made the space loud, and he had to speak up to be heard over it.

"Please, call me Julia." Theo ushered them into the room. It wasn't large, and a counter stretched around three sides. On one side was a microscope and slides, and the other two were filled with various kinds plants under powerful grow lights. "This looks really interesting."

"Thank you." Theo smiled. "It's pretty fun. Actually—" He picked up his phone, which was on the counter. "It's just about feeding time. Would you like to watch?"

Julia wasn't sure what he meant, but she nodded uncertainly.

Theo went to a small refrigerator under the counter and pulled a plastic bag out of the narrow freezer compartment. Then he used tweezers to pull out a—oh dear. He took a frozen cricket out of the bag and carried it to a plant on the far counter.

"Is that a—"

"Venus flytrap." Theo was grinning. "Watch this."

Julia felt a little queasy as he set the dead cricket in one of the open mouths—there was probably a more official name, but Julia didn't know what it was—and moved the dead bug around a bit. Then he quickly pulled back as the spiky mouth snapped shut.

"Pretty cool, huh?" Theo was clearly pleased with the plant's trick.

"That's something," Julia said. She tried to be enthusiastic. The cricket was already dead, after all. It hadn't felt any pain as the plant's jaws snapped shut around it. But there was still something that felt wrong about how excited Theo had been to watch that cricket get eaten. "Wow."

"They don't get fed very often, so you came at just the right time."

Professor Elmore cleared his throat and said, "Julia, why don't you tell Theo about the plants you found?"

"Right." Julia reached into her purse and pulled out her phone. She opened the photos app and scrolled to the pictures she'd taken in Forsyth Park. "I came across these plants in Forsyth Park the other day," she said, holding out a photo of the secret garden.

Theo took the phone and used two fingers to enlarge the picture. His eyes widened. "You found this *where*?"

"In Forsyth Park."

"Wow. For real?" He studied the photo, moving the picture around so he could see different parts of it. "That's angel's-trumpet. From the family solanaceae. That contains significant quantities of tropane alkaloids, much like datura and black henbane."

"So…that's poisonous, right?"

"For sure. I mean, it's mostly used as a hallucinogenic, because ingesting the plant can cause crazy visions. But it can also cause paralysis, tachycardia, memory loss, and death."

"Yikes. And yet people take it on purpose?"

Theo shrugged. "Chasing that elusive high. You'd be surprised what people will do for access to mind-altering drugs."

The professor cleared his throat again.

"You've also got foxglove here," Theo continued quickly. "Digitalis. That's been used medicinally for centuries. There's a chemical in it called digoxin that's used to treat cardiac arrythmia today, but over the years it's been used to treat all kinds of things, including epilepsy."

"But it's poisonous too, right?"

"Oh yes. Very much so. It can cause vomiting, changes to vision, convulsions, even death."

"But…" Julia tried to understand. "It can do all that, but it's also used medicinally?"

"The difference is in how you use it, isn't it?" Theo smiled. "Here's a fun fact. I mentioned changes in vision. Digitalis can cause halos around light in your sight, and it can also cause your sight to give objects a yellow tinge. It's speculated that Van Gogh was using digitalis to treat his epilepsy during his 'yellow period.' You can see the evidence of the halos around spots of light in his famous painting *Starry Night*."

"Wow." Julia hadn't known that. The information put a whole different spin on the famous painter's work.

"And that's atropa belladonna. I've got that here." He pointed to a plant with small purple flowers on the counter behind him, and then turned back and moved to a different part of the screen. "And is that monkshood? And datura? Wow. You found all of these in one place?"

"I told you he knew poisonous plants." Professor Elmore was smiling, his arms crossed over his chest.

"Yes, they were all just planted there together," Julia confirmed. "I was concerned, because a garden full of poisonous plants doesn't seem to belong in a public park."

"Oh no." Theo shook his head. "No, that's a terrible idea. These plants are really dangerous. But how cool is that?"

Julia wasn't sure she followed his logic.

"I'm trying to figure out where they might have come from," Julia said.

"I'd like to know that too. Whoever planted them definitely knows their poisonous plants. I'd like to meet this person. And I've never seen Aconitum that deep purple. I want to know where they got it."

"Aconitum?" Julia repeated.

"From the family Ranunculaceae. Commonly known as monkshood, wolfsbane, devil's helmet, blue rocket, or queen of poisons."

"Do you have any thoughts on how those plants might have ended up in Forsyth Park?" Professor Elmore asked. "You always seem to know the people who are into this sort of thing."

"I thought I did." Theo shrugged. "I hadn't heard of any of my buddies pulling a stunt like this, but I can ask around on the message boards, see if anyone knows anything."

"That would be wonderful," Julia said.

Professor Elmore escorted Julia out of Theo's lab shortly after that, but before she left the building he stopped and said, "He's really a good kid. I know he comes across as a little...intense. He has what some might consider an unusual passion. But he's been through a lot, and he's really incredibly smart and wouldn't hurt a fly."

Julia wasn't so sure. She'd just seen him delight in feeding a plant known for attracting flies specifically to kill them. But she just nodded and thanked Professor Elmore for his time and drove away, trying to sort out everything she'd just heard and seen.

***

Julia and Beau were loading the dishwasher after dinner when the doorbell rang. Beau went to answer it while Julia set the serving bowls and plates in the rack and started the machine. Beau was chatting with whoever was at the door, but that didn't tell her much about who it was. Beau would chat with the UPS driver, the Girl Scout selling cookies, or someone who had come to the wrong address altogether. They would all leave feeling like they'd made a new friend. So Julia was surprised when, a few minutes later, Beau led Cassie into the kitchen. Her red hair was pulled back into a messy ponytail, and she was wearing a long gauzy skirt and tank top that showed off her trim arms. All that yoga really paid off, apparently. Julia tried to fight her initial instinct, which was to brace herself for whatever disappointment Cassie was about to bring. She hated that that was still how she reacted to her sister, but it took time to rebuild trust. And there was a lot to rebuild.

"Hi there!" Cassie pulled a piece of paper out of her knit cross-body purse. "I wanted to drop off this sponsorship form for the 5K. You can have your sponsors fill out their pledges here."

Oh dear. Julia thought she'd have more time to prepare for this.

"Thank you for bringing it by." Julia looked around and saw that Beau had vanished. No doubt trying to be thoughtful to leave them to talk, which was sweet, but meant he would be no help here. "But I'm afraid I'm not going to be able to do the race after all."

There. She'd done it. "I'll still make a donation," she added quickly when she saw how Cassie's face fell. "I want to support the school however I can. But I just don't think running is for me."

"Oh." Cassie pressed her lips together. "Okay."

"I'm really glad you asked me," Julia said. "It's just, I went out on a run this morning, and it was awful. I don't think I'm cut out for this."

Cassie nodded, but Julia could see she was disappointed. She wanted to not let herself care. Julia had been disappointed by Cassie for decades, and while part of her wished she could simply not let herself be affected, she couldn't.

"Running is hard, at first," Cassie said. "But I know you can do it. We could train together, if you want."

Now Julia felt anger start to flare up. Why couldn't Cassie just accept Julia's no? It was so like Cassie to only hear what she wanted to hear.

"Try. Please? For the girls?" Cassie set the entry form down on the counter. "They look up to you so much. It would mean a lot to them. And what kind of example would it be to them if you backed out just because it was hard?"

Julia was pretty certain she was being manipulated. That was Cassie's specialty. Well, that and running away to let other people clean up the messes she left behind. But Julia couldn't figure out a way to answer her that didn't sound ridiculous.

"I bet that once your body gets used to running, you'll start to enjoy it. It does so much to help relieve stress."

If that was true, Julia was going to need to a take a nice long run after this conversation.

"I know it's hard, Jules," Cassie said. Something in her voice had changed. "But please. Can't we do it together?"

Together. They hadn't really done anything together—not in any meaningful way—since before Julia went off to college. But that was decades ago, and over that time, Julia had learned to build up her defenses to avoid having her heart broken again and again. She knew better than to believe Cassie. She wasn't trustworthy. She would get distracted when the next thing came along, leaving Julia holding the bag. She didn't think about the chaos, or the people, she left in her wake.

But still, this was her sister, whom Julia had held in bed when she'd had nightmares when they were girls. This was her sister, who had held on to Julia's hand and wouldn't let it go as Julia walked her into elementary school for the first time. Who'd sat with Julia at the end of the dock, their legs dangling in the water, giggling about boys. Julia knew better than to trust Cassie, but she couldn't quite bring herself to ignore the love she felt for her, despite it all.

"I'll help you," Cassie said.

All the excuses Julia had prepared flew out of her mind. She'd been certain she was done. She'd had no intention of running that race five minutes ago, and every shred of experience taught her to know better than to trust Cassie. But somehow, now that Cassie was here, begging her, Julia heard herself say, "Okay."

***

Julia and Beau were reading in bed when Julia's phone rang. Meredith's name flashed on the screen. Beau glanced up from his biography of Lyndon Johnson, his reading glasses perched on his nose. Julia set down her mystery and picked up her phone from the bedside table. "Hello?"

"The kids are finally in bed. They wanted to do a Star Wars marathon, but I cut it off after *The Empire Strikes Back*."

Julia smiled. She knew where this was going. "Now that the kids are in bed, you're looking for an update, right?"

"Naturally. I wouldn't trade the time with my grandkids for anything, but I have to admit I'm jealous that you got to have all the fun investigating those plants today."

"I'm not sure I would call it fun...."

"Let's start with suspects. Who's on the list?"

"First up, there's Calvin Corliss. Randy Torrez, who works at the park, mentioned him. He works for the parks department but doesn't have any business in Forsyth Park, and yet he's been spotted there several times in recent weeks. He was arrested for drunk driving back in 2015, and I asked Carmen to pull any other court records that pertain to him. There wasn't much online, but we'll need to do more research into him."

"He sounds like a solid lead. Nice work."

"Then we have Elyse Cheney. She's a gardener that my friend Jan pointed me to. Jan told me Elyse knows a lot about hemlock, but Elyse denied it up and down. Says Jan must have been mistaken. The thing is, I'm almost positive she was lying."

"Why?"

"I can't say, exactly. Just...she seemed like she was lying."

"We'll need to get more than that, I'm afraid. Have you done any background research on her?"

"Not yet. She told me she's from a fishing village in Cornwall—she's British—and she and her husband Bryce lived in Chicago for a while, but that's really all I know."

"Any chance she's lying about being British too?"

"Not much. She served me tea. As in, hot tea. Earl Grey."

"In June?"

"Yeah, like I said, I'm pretty sure she's British."

"Okay. I believe you. Who else?"

"Jan put me in touch with someone at the Savannah Botanical Gardens, who put me in touch with a biology professor at Savannah

State, who introduced me to a student named Theo Williams. He's working on a senior project about poisonous plants and he seemed... Well, just a little...off."

"Off how?"

"He was excited to feed his Venus flytrap."

"Gross, but not against the law."

"And he knew a whole lot about the plants in the photo. Like...a *lot*."

"Well, you just said he's studying them. So that doesn't seem too strange."

"No, but there's just... Something felt strange. And just as I was leaving, his professor mentioned that he was a good kid, but he'd been through a lot. I wanted to follow up on that but haven't had a chance."

"Theo Williams, added to the list," Meredith said. "Who else?"

"Well..." Julia thought for a moment. "That's it, for now."

"Okay. That's a good list of suspects to start with. What do we have for clues?"

"Not much yet. Only the garden itself. Just before I discovered the plants, I saw movement, so I think someone was back there, but I couldn't say anything about them or where they went. There was no one there when I got there."

"We need to get that security camera footage," Meredith said. "Both from the park and from the neighbors."

"If the neighbors have any."

"Those cameras are becoming so common now, I bet someone at that end of the park has something. I'll bring the kids in tomorrow, and they can help us go door-to-door."

"Are you sure? You're supposed to have the day off."

"It'll be good to get them out of the house. I don't think I can handle too many more lightsabers."

"That will be helpful, then."

"We should also talk to Rhonda Sullivan."

It took Julia a moment to follow. "At the diner. Because of her dog."

"Right. She said her dog got sick after a walk in the park. We should find out where she was in the park. Maybe she saw something."

"Good idea." And then, after a moment's thought, Julia said, "The poisonous plants are back behind a fence and through bushes. Dogs aren't supposed to go behind the fences." There were signs all over the park to keep dogs on leashes except in marked areas.

"Dog owners let their dogs roam off-leash all over that park. You know that as well as I do," Meredith said.

"Fair enough."

"Let's take the kids to lunch at the diner. They'll love it, and it will give us a chance to talk to Rhonda."

"That sounds like a good plan."

"Hopefully when we do some more digging on these leads, we'll quickly get to the truth."

Julia wished she had Meredith's optimism.

Chapter Five

JULIA WOKE UP SORE WEDNESDAY morning. She rolled out of bed, groaning, and then popped an Advil along with her breakfast. Every muscle in her body seemed to hurt.

By the time she got into the office, she was feeling a bit better. She sat down at her computer and followed up on a few cases she was working on and answered some emails, and then she began by researching Elyse Cheney. She started with a general internet search, which didn't reveal much aside from an Instagram account that featured lots of shots of her garden.

Julia knew where she lived, so she did some research into the house, and while she found that it had cost even more than she had expected, she wasn't at all surprised to find out that it was expensive. She looked into Bryce Cheney and found the name of the commercial real estate firm he worked for, but there wasn't a lot to learn about him, as far as she could tell. He'd grown up in Connecticut, gone to Duke, and started working. There was nothing about either of them that mentioned poison or dangerous flowers. Nothing to explain what Elyse was lying about or why.

Julia knew the moment Meredith and the kids arrived. They burst in through the front door, chattering away, and the clatter of busy feet on the floorboards was unmistakable. Julia heard Carmen talking to the kids for a minute, and then they started to move down the hallway. Julia stood and walked to the doorway.

"Hello there."

"Hi!" Kinsley was wearing a pink T-shirt that said SMILE IF YOU LOVE UNICORNS over darker pink shorts, and her blond hair was pushed back with a unicorn headband.

"Hello! You got your ears pierced," Julia observed.

"Mom took me as an end-of-school celebration." Kinsley leaned forward so Julia could get a better look at the sparkly studs.

"They look great. Very grown-up."

Kinsley beamed.

"And how are you, Kaden?" The eleven-year-old had copper-colored hair and a sprinkling of freckles across his cheeks.

"Hi." He looked at her and then looked away. Julia knew his parents had been working with him on making eye contact, and technically, he had done so.

"These two are my helpers for the day," Meredith said. "Are you still up for trying to find doorbell cam footage?"

"Sure am," Julia said.

"Perfect. And I found something last night I thought you might be interested in seeing."

"What's that?"

"I'll email it to you as soon as I get to my desk."

"All right." Julia's curiosity was piqued. "Go, then."

"I'll send it. I'm just going to check on a few things and we'll be ready to go. How does twenty minutes sound?"

"Perfect."

Julia went back to her computer, and a few minutes later, an email from Meredith popped up. It was a link to an article in the *Telegraph*, a newspaper in Macon, from four years back. *Teen suspected in poisoning*, the headline read. Well, now. This was interesting.

> *Courtney Sosby, 17, was rushed to the hospital Saturday night after ingesting a berry from what is suspected to be a poisonous atropa belladonna plant. The plant was said to be located in the home of Sosby's boyfriend, Theo Williams, also 17, who was found to have a collection of plants considered to be toxic. Sosby claimed Williams had encouraged her to eat the berry and she did so, not knowing it was toxic.*

Julia scrolled down, looking for the rest of the article, but a box popped up, asking her to log in to read the rest of the article.

Julia got up and walked to Meredith's office. "It's behind a paywall. Were you able to read it?"

"Unfortunately, no." Meredith looked up from her screen. "I think we'll have to go to the library to see if we can find the rest of the article. But he poisoned his girlfriend."

"*Allegedly* poisoned his girlfriend," Julia said. "We don't know what really happened."

"Right," Meredith said, though she didn't seem convinced.

"I mean, he's not locked up or anything, so we have to allow for some doubt," Julia said.

"I'll keep an open mind," Meredith insisted. "But I want to try to get to the library to read the rest of the article today."

Julia hated to wait. She wanted to find out what had happened to Theo—and what had happened to his girlfriend—now.

"Should we do that instead of trying to get security camera footage?" Julia suggested.

"I say we stick with the plan and hit up the library after lunch," Meredith said.

"That sounds fine." Julia went back to her office and returned a few emails. Twenty minutes later, she walked over to Meredith's office again. Kinsley was drawing an elaborate scene involving unicorns on a yellow legal pad, and Kaden had gotten into the supply closet and was now using colorful packs of Post-Its to build an intricately constructed tower.

"Ready?"

"Let's go."

"Do I have to go?" Kaden added a turquoise pack to the stack.

"Fresh air will be good for you."

Kaden didn't look happy, but he didn't argue with his grandmother.

A few minutes later, they were crossing the street and heading toward the park. Kinsley skipped ahead, headed for the playground on the east side of the park, but she kept stopping to look at chipmunks. Meredith corralled her, and they eventually made their way up to the northwest corner of the park to where the garden had been found.

"Okay. So let's target the buildings along this end of Whitaker," Julia said. "And also on Gaston along the whole length of the park."

Meredith nodded. "Bull Street dead-ends at the entrance to the park there. We can see if anyone at that end of the street might have anything useful as well."

"That sounds like a plan."

They followed the path and then crossed the lawn to the edge of the park and stood along Whitaker Street. The Magnolia Investigations office was just down the road a few blocks but out of sight now.

"Should we start with the animal hospital?" Julia asked.

"Seems like a good place to begin," Meredith agreed.

"Do they have dogs there? I love dogs. I want to get a golden retriever, but Daddy won't let me. Did you know golden retrievers have webbed paws? That's how they can swim so well. The other day I wanted to design the perfect dog for surfing, so I thought you could cross a corgi with a dachshund, because dachshunds have short legs and long bodies, and the corgi has a sleek coat. And then you could cross that with a golden retriever, which has a sleek coat plus an otter-like tail and webbed paws and you'd get a *redachsadorgie*, which would be prefect for surfing."

Kinsley chatted nonstop as they crossed Whitaker and approached the Italianate mansion with the rounded portico, fluted columns, and wrought iron balconies. It was the most stunning animal hospital Julia had ever seen. Then again, so many places in Savannah were like that. It was simply a beautiful town, so full of historic buildings that even animal clinics looked like movie sets.

They walked up the steps and under the porch and inside the lobby, which was set with sand-colored tile and painted a soft blue. Colorful paintings of dogs and cats hung on the walls. It looked like a slightly classier version of any other vet clinic she'd ever seen.

"Hello." Meredith walked up to the front desk and smiled at the young woman behind the counter. Kinsley had already wandered over to a woman with a chihuahua on a leash and was making friends with the little dog. "I'm Meredith Bellefontaine, and this is Julia Foley. We run Magnolia Investigations, just down the street."

"Hi there." The woman had straight black hair and wore a name tag that said JEN. "I remember you." She smiled at Julia. "You brought in a cat. Did you end up keeping her?"

"We did." Julia had accidentally hit Bunny with her car and had brought her here for treatment before eventually taking her home.

"How's she doing?"

"Bunny's doing great. She's just the sweetest cat."

"Oh I'm so glad." Jen smiled up at them. "Did you need something for Bunny?"

"Actually, we're hoping you can help us with something," Meredith said. "We're investigating an incident that happened in the park, and we're hoping to gather security camera footage from businesses that face the park."

"Oh dear. An incident?"

They had decided to try to be as vague as possible when they talked about what they were investigating, to try to avoid tipping off anyone who might know more than they let on.

"We think someone probably came and went several times over the course of the past few weeks," Julia said. "We wondered whether it would be possible to take a look at your security camera footage for that time frame."

"I'll have to check with Dr. Preston," Jen said. "But I'm sure he'll want to help."

"Thank you so much." Julia slid a business card across the counter. "We really appreciate it."

They turned to go and had to pry Kinsley away from the chihuahua, who was happily letting her hold it. Then they headed back out onto the street and went to the next building, which was a private three-story home, with tall windows and light blue shutters.

"Maybe we should divide and conquer here," Meredith suggested, and Julia agreed. Meredith took Kaden with her to talk to the owners at that house, and Julia and Kinsley went to the next house, which was a French colonial with large porches, dripping in white trim, off both levels of the front. No one answered the door, but Julia left a note and her business card and slipped it under the door. She saw that they had a smart doorbell, with a camera built right in, so she waved at it. There was no telling whether the owners would respond, but she hoped that appearing friendly on the footage would help. On the corner was the tan building that housed the Savannah Historical Society. Meredith had been the president of the historical society for many years, so they didn't even bother to stop in now. Meredith knew there was no security camera on the building.

They then turned onto Gaston Street, where they stopped in at another private home that had a hair salon on the basement level. The salon owner said the homeowners had installed a security system recently, and she promised to see if she could get footage from them. Next was a brick-fronted building that was a dorm for students at the Savannah College of Art and Design, which had buildings all over town, including several that fronted Forsyth Park.

On the corner of Gaston and Bull Streets, Julia and Kinsley came to the Oglethorpe Club, a plainer building in the neighborhood that housed one of the oldest and most exclusive private clubs in the country. Beau had some friends who were members, but the club had always seemed unfriendly and kind of snooty to Julia. The tuxedoed man who stood by the door agreed to pass on a business card to the management, but Julia didn't hold out much hope that they would hear back from the Club, though she was certain that an establishment like that would have security cameras.

They stopped in at a few more houses along Gaston and those just up Bull Street, and then, on the corner of Gaston and Drayton, they stood in front of the Candler Oak, a three-hundred-year-old tree that was protected and cared for by citizens of Savannah. Behind it was an old hospital building that had treated patients during the Civil War and was now owned by the Savannah College of Art and Design. Meredith and Kaden met up with them there.

"SCAD must have cameras everywhere," Julia said. "What do you think? Should we see if they'll give us their footage?"

"I suppose it can't hurt to ask," Meredith said. "But I don't even know where we'd start."

"When are we going to be *done*?" Kaden asked.

"I'm hungry," Kinsley whined. The kids had been slowing down, and Julia was worried that the women would soon face a full-on meltdown, so she said, "Why don't we do some research on the best way to request that from the university? In the meantime, maybe it's time to take a break and get lunch."

"Yes!" Kinsley jumped up and punched the air.

It was a short walk to the Downhome Diner, where they were quickly seated in a booth. Julia loved the comfortable Southern charm of this place, especially the prints showing historical pictures of Savannah that hung on the walls. Today they sat under the picture of Fort Jackson on the banks of the Savannah River.

"I want grilled cheese and French fries," Kinsley said without even opening the menu. "And a chocolate milkshake."

"Burger," Kaden said. He pulled a pen out of his pocket and proceeded to draw a series of interconnected cubes on a paper placemat.

"Hi there." Justine, a waitress with dark-framed glasses and a big smile greeted them, sliding a handful of silverware and napkins onto the table. "Welcome, welcome. I see we have some special visitors today."

"These are my grandkids." Meredith was beaming. "Kaden and Kinsley."

"Hi!" Kinsley smiled at Justine.

"Hello." Kaden glanced up quickly and then down.

"Here are some menus," Justine said, picking them up from a stack on a nearby stand and sliding them across the table. "The special is shrimp and grits, so you all came on the right day. I'll leave you to look over the menu, and just let me know if you need anything."

Julia already knew she was going to order the special. Maribelle made it with bacon crumbled on top, and Justine was only exaggerating a bit when she said it was to die for. She closed the menu and looked around, and she was glad to see that Rhonda was working today.

When Justine came back and brought glasses of water, they placed their orders. Kinsley then launched into a monologue about a television show she liked about puppies who go to school, and she barely took a breath until Charlene King Jackson, owner of the diner and the daughter of their friend Maggie Lu, appeared at the table.

"Hello there. I wanted to say hello and give a special welcome to my two favorite mini detectives."

"We're not detectives *yet*," Kinsley said. Kaden looked up briefly and then went back to drawing his squares.

"It's good to see you," Julia said. "How are you?"

"Good. This place keeps me hopping, and that's a good thing."

"I'm glad to hear it." The diner was still relatively new, and Charlene had worked hard to make it one of the best dining destinations in town.

They chatted for a few minutes, and then Charlene said, "Is there anything I can do for you all?"

"Actually, we'd love to talk with Rhonda when she gets a moment," Meredith said. "Last time I was here, she mentioned that her dog was sick, and I wanted to ask her about it."

"I'll send her on over," Charlene said. "You all enjoy your meal. Your food should be out in just a few moments."

A few minutes later Rhonda appeared at the table. Julia guessed she was in her fifties or so. "Hello there," Rhonda said. "Charlene said you asked to talk to me?"

"Yes," Julia said. "We wanted to hear how your dog was doing. Meredith says he was sick."

"That's right. Dude got real sick last week," Rhonda said. "But he's doing much better now."

"Your dog is named *Dude*?" Kinsley laughed.

Rhonda shrugged. "He's the only dude in my life."

Kinsley found this response hilarious, and as she dissolved into giggles, Meredith said, "I'm glad to hear he's doing better. You told me you'd recently been in Forsyth Park when he got sick?"

Rhonda nodded. "That's right. That's the only thing I can think of that was different on that day. Otherwise, it was just a normal day."

"Where in the park did you go?" Julia asked.

"Dude likes to walk, so we went all over the place," Rhonda said. "That dog is ten years old, and I can barely keep up."

"Did you go to the northwest corner of the park?" Julia asked.

Seeing her blank look, Julia quickly added, "The Whitaker Street side of the park, by the historical society."

"Oh right. Sure, we were up that way."

Julia picked up a straw and tapped it on the table to pull the paper down. "Was Dude off his leash at any point?"

Rhonda looked around, as if making sure no one listening in. "Are you secretly working for the park police or something?"

Julia could see that she was joking, mostly.

"Are there really park police?" Kinsley asked, eyes wide.

"No such thing," Kaden said. "The parks are maintained by the Parks and Recreation Department."

Rhonda shook her head and laughed. "That settles that, I guess."

"We found a hidden garden in the park a few days ago," Julia told her. "It was back behind a bunch of azaleas, with a fence in front of them."

"Yep." Rhonda was nodding. "I know exactly where you mean. Dude was back there, all right. He's a Jack Russell terrier, so he's small, but that boy can jump. He hopped that fence like it was nothing and then he ran off and vanished behind the bushes. He wouldn't come when I called him either, so eventually I gave up and hiked my leg up over that fence and went after him. Let me tell you, it's a good thing there was no one else around, else I might have ended up in one of those viral videos. *Crazy lady falls trying to climb over fence.* It was not graceful, that's for sure."

Julia hated to hear Rhonda be self-deprecating, even when it was meant as a joke. But she didn't know how to respond, and Rhonda rushed on.

"It was one of those iron ones, with the points on top every few feet? Nearly stabbed myself a few times, but I finally got over. Then I had to push my way through the bushes. It was like I was a real explorer or something. Anyway, once I survived that, I got back into this crazy hidden garden with some of the most beautiful flowers I've ever seen. I couldn't believe it and figured they must have hidden all the best spots so you have to really work to find them. But was Dude enjoying the foliage? No he was not. He was chewing on one of the plants. Actually, I guess you could say he was enjoying it, in some ways. Anyway, I shooed him away and got him back over the fence, and after that I put his leash back on."

Julia met Meredith's eye, and Meredith nodded.

"I think that explains it," Meredith said. "I'm afraid the plants he found were poisonous."

"Poisonous?" Rhonda repeated. "What? That beautiful garden?"

"I'm afraid so. Dude must have chewed on the one of the toxic plants."

"Why would they plant poisonous flowers in the park?" Rhonda pushed herself up and crossed her arms over her chest.

"The Parks and Recreation Department"—Meredith glanced at Kaden, who nodded—"didn't. They didn't know it was there. We're actually trying to figure out how those plants ended up there."

"In that case, I hope you find the person soon," Rhonda said. "And they should take those plants out before someone else gets hurt." She put her hands on her hips. "What if Dude had eaten enough to kill him?"

"They're working on taking them out," Julia said. "We were wondering, did you see anyone back there? Or did you see anything that struck you as odd?"

"Other than a secret garden full of poisonous flowers?" Rhonda said sarcastically. "No, I'm afraid I didn't notice anything else that struck me as odd."

Julia tried not to be disappointed. It had been a long shot, she knew. The bell on the serving window dinged, and Rhonda turned her head. "Well, unless you have any more questions, I'd better get back to it," she said.

"Thank you for your help. We appreciate it," Meredith said.

"You let me know if you find out anything more, you hear?" Rhonda said. They promised they would, and she turned away. A few minutes later Justine brought their meals to the table. The shrimp and grits were as good as Justine had promised, Kinsley pronounced the grilled cheese "awesomtastic," and they were all talking of being stuffed when they stepped out onto Whitaker Street again.

"So," Julia said, "are you still up for the library?"

Both kids cheered, and they all piled into Meredith's car and made the short drive to the Carnegie Library.

"Why don't you get started with the research terminals, while I get these two settled in the children's section," Meredith said once they got inside the building. "And then I'll come find you."

"That sounds great," Julia said. The library was not too crowded today, and Julia made her way over to the research terminals. She clicked on the icon for a database of newspaper and magazine articles from around the country. She and Meredith had used it many times in their cases, so she knew how to navigate the system quickly.

She typed in the words THEO WILLIAMS and THE TELEGRAPH, and the full article Julia had started earlier came up.

Courtney Sosby, 17, was rushed to the hospital Saturday night after ingesting a berry from what is suspected to be a poisonous atropa belladonna plant. The plant was said to be located in the home of Sosby's boyfriend, Theo Williams, also 17, who was found to have a collection of plants considered to be toxic. Sosby claimed Williams had encouraged her to eat the berry and she did so, not knowing it was toxic. Williams was brought in for questioning and charged with poisoning not resulting in death. Williams is being held at the county jail until further notice.

In addition to the plants that contain toxic properties, the police also found several marijuana plants, which were confiscated. Williams also faces felony charges for the possession of the illegal plants.

Well. The wooden chair creaked beneath Julia as she sat back. So Theo had poisoned his girlfriend—*allegedly* poisoned his girlfriend, she added mentally—and had also been found in possession of marijuana plants, all before he'd graduated from high school. No wonder Professor Elmore had said Theo had faced some trouble in his past.

But was it true? Had he been convicted of poisoning his girlfriend? He had, it seemed, owned the toxic plants. But did that mean he'd given them to her to ingest? Less important for this investigation, but still relevant, was the fact that he'd been growing marijuana plants, which were totally illegal in the state of Georgia. The crime carried a minimum sentence of one year in prison, Julia knew.

What had happened to Theo's girlfriend? Julia couldn't go on without knowing whether she was all right. She opened an internet search window and typed in the name COURTNEY SOSBY. There were pages of results, and it took some time to narrow it down, but Julia finally found an Instagram page for a Courtney Sosby whose bio said she was from a small town in Georgia. There were selfies of a blond girl with a high ponytail and big sunglasses on a dock jutting into a lake, and with a guitar, and also several photos of a street with lots of neon lights. From the pictures and captions on the site, Julia surmised that Courtney was now living in Nashville, and seemed to be pursuing a career in music. If this was the right Courtney Sosby, it seemed she had survived the incident relatively unscathed.

Now that her mind was at ease, Julia clicked back to the page of search results she'd found and clicked on the next line that came up. *Poisoned Girlfriend Released from Hospital,* the next headline read, and Julia read that Courtney had recovered and returned home. Theo had apologized for the incident but denied responsibility for Courtney's ingesting the poison.

The next article began with the headline *Williams, Facing Drug Charges, Denies Intent to Sell Marijuana*. Julia scanned the article. Theo had apparently said he didn't use the marijuana or sell or give it away—he claimed he was interested in the plants for their unique chemical structure and was interested in learning about their specific growth pattern.

Julia shook her head. Had he really thought people would believe that? If a defendant had come into her courtroom with an excuse that flimsy, she would have had a hard time not laughing out loud.

Williams Accepts Plea Deal, the next headline read. The article was from three months after the first article. Julia clicked on it and read the article, which said that Theo had pled guilty to both the poisoning and the drug possession charge and was given a year of probation.

"What did you find?" Meredith sat down in the chair beside her.

"He pled guilty to poisoning his girlfriend," Julia said.

"So he did it? He actually poisoned her?"

"Not necessarily," Julia said. "He took a plea deal, and there are all kinds of reasons people do that. Sometimes they truly are guilty, but sometimes their lawyer convinces them making a deal is their best shot at avoiding jail time or facing lesser punishment."

"But why would someone plead guilty when they aren't?"

"In many cases, to avoid a trial. Trials are expensive, invasive, and if you lose, the penalties can be far worse. There are all kinds of reasons his lawyers might have wanted to avoid a trial, so they might have encouraged him to accept the deal."

"Or, there's always the chance that he pled guilty because he was guilty."

"That's the other possibility. He also pled guilty to the drug possession charge, and—"

"The what now?"

"Right. So it wasn't just poisoning his girlfriend that got Theo in trouble. It turned out, he wasn't just growing poisonous plants, he was also growing marijuana. He said he wasn't intending to smoke it himself or to sell it, he was just interested in how the plants grow."

Meredith laughed out loud, earning her several annoyed looks from fellow library patrons.

"Sorry. What I meant was, that sounds unlikely."

"I agree. And he should have faced a year of jail for it, but he got probation instead."

"Why is that?"

"Hard to say." Julia shrugged. "I'm sure avoiding jail time was part of the plea deal. The fact that he was a minor no doubt factored into it too. And if it was a first offense…"

Julia had been a judge in juvenile court, and she believed jail time often did more harm than good in young people, depending on the severity of what they had done.

"Okay. So we know Theo has a passion for growing poisonous plants and that he poisoned his girlfriend—"

"Allegedly poisoned his girlfriend. We don't know what really happened."

"Pled guilty to poisoning his girlfriend, then. I'd say he seems like a prime candidate for our garden mystery."

"He's definitely high on the list," Julia admitted. "Though as far as I know, none of the plants in that garden were marijuana."

"It would have been too obvious to plant that in a public place, though, right?" Meredith said. "That's a pretty recognizable plant, and comes with heavy penalties. There's nothing illegal, per se, about having any of the other plants in that garden. It's just that having them all planted together, and in a public park, leads to a lot of questions."

"And potentially disastrous situations."

"Is there a way to find out exactly what happened in the discussion of his plea deal?" Meredith asked.

"Criminal records are public records," Julia said. "So yes, we could get a hold of them."

"What's the quickest way to do that?" Meredith asked. "Filing of FOIA requests takes forever."

Meredith was right that requesting records under the Freedom of Information Act protocol could be a lengthy process.

"A normal person would go to the courthouse in Bibb County— that's where Macon is—and file for the records."

"But how would someone do it if, say, they had been a judge in the state of Georgia?"

"Let me ask some friends for help. I'll see if I can speed up the process."

"Hello there. I thought I saw you two come in."

Julia looked up and smiled when she saw Maggie Lu. She was wearing a flowered dress with a high neck and long skirt.

"Hello, Maggie Lu," Meredith said. "How are you today?"

"I'm doing well. And you?"

"We're both doing all right," Meredith said. "Are my grandkids causing trouble?"

"Those sweet children in the kids' section are yours?"

Meredith nodded.

"They're adorable. And they're angels. They're both curled up on the beanbag chairs with books."

"I'm glad to hear it," Meredith said.

"And what kind of case are you working on today?" Maggie Lu nodded at the screen.

"We're trying to find out who is growing poisonous plants in Forsyth Park," Julia said.

"Poisonous plants? Really?"

"Really," Meredith said. "Several varieties, all planted together in a hidden garden behind some bushes in Forsyth Park. We're trying to find out who planted them and why."

"And to get them removed before someone gets hurt," Julia added.

"What kind of plants?" Maggie Lu asked.

"Datura, belladonna, foxglove, angel's-trumpet, hemlock…maybe some others." Julia hadn't known a thing about any of these plants until recently, but now she was listing them off like a pro.

"Is that right?"

Julia glanced at Meredith, who was looking up at Maggie Lu.

"Maggie Lu, you look like you've got an idea," Meredith said.

"As a matter of fact, I do. I was just thinking, there's a book we have that might help."

"Is it a book about poisonous plants?" Julia asked.

"It's actually about the medicinal properties of plants. Tinctures, herbs, that kind of thing. It was written by a woman who was an herbalist in Haiti in the early part of the twentieth century. But it mentions some of the plants you're talking about."

"It could be worth taking a look at," Meredith said.

Julia nodded, though she wasn't so sure how much it would help. They were looking for poisonous plants, not plants that helped people. But Julia knew better than to dismiss any lead their librarian friend thought to give them. She was a researcher extraordinaire.

"Let me see if I can find it," Maggie Lu said. She turned and walked back toward the reference desk.

"I'll see if there are any more articles that mention Theo Williams," Julia said, and turned back to the computer screen in front of her. Meredith scooted over a bit so she was looking at the next computer terminal. Julia opened a search window but didn't find much; once Theo's plea bargain was reached, the story dropped from the papers. If they wanted to find out more about that story, they would need to look elsewhere.

She leaned back and stretched her arms up, stifling a yawn. Maybe it was time for some coffee. She craned her neck, looking for Maggie Lu, but she was out of sight. Maybe Julia could convince Meredith to stop and grab coffee before they went back to the office.

Then she heard Meredith gasp.

"What is it?" Julia craned her neck, and she saw that Meredith was looking at some kind of garden on the screen.

"Remember how you thought Elyse Cheney was lying?"

Julia nodded.

"Well, you were right."

Chapter Six

"WHAT DID YOU FIND?" JULIA scooted her chair closer, but all she saw on the screen was a walled garden of some sort.

"I decided to do some digging on Elyse. Either Jan was mistaken about her knowledge of hemlock, or Elyse was hiding what she knew." And then, after a pause, she added, "Plus, who serves hot tea in June in Georgia?"

"I think British people have hot tea just about all the time."

"Well, whatever. I ran a search for her name in the newspaper database, and her name came up in an article from the *Northumberland Gazette*."

The name vaguely registered. Had Elyse mentioned Northumberland?

"The article is about a fundraiser for the Alnwyck Garden, which is apparently a lovely garden in the region. It looks quite nice. They have beautiful cherry blossoms, a rose garden, mini golf, even a restaurant in a treehouse. The kids would love that."

"That's right. She mentioned that she'd worked at a garden on the grounds of a castle there," Julia said.

"This is it. And here's what Elyse had to say." Meredith clicked over to the newspaper article and leaned forward to read off the screen. "'We are grateful for the continued support of our neighbors and patrons, and a successful event will allow us to create even more meaningful experiences for generations to come,' said Elyse Cheney, Head Gardener."

"Okay." Julia didn't see what was so inflammatory yet.

"But get this. I was looking at the website for Alnwyck Gardens, and they also have a Poison Garden."

"A what?"

"It's crazy. Look at this."

Julia nudged her chair even closer, and Meredith clicked on a link that said POISON GARDEN. An image of a garden, walled off with iron fencing, appeared on the screen. An arched sign over the gates announced THE POISON GARDEN, and on the gates themselves, there were signs with skulls and crossbones saying THESE PLANTS CAN KILL.

"What in the world?" Julia tried to wrap her head around this. "It's a garden specifically planted with poisonous plants?"

"Apparently," Meredith said. "Lots of them."

"Why would anyone want to cultivate a poison garden?"

"It says here that all of Alnwyck Garden is the brainchild of the Duchess of Northumberland, who opened the garden on the castle grounds to give something back to the neighborhood."

"How generous."

Meredith ignored her and continued. "The poison garden is contained within the old walled garden of the castle. The duchess apparently decided that instead of having an herb garden, she wanted something more interesting."

"I'd say she succeeded."

"The garden contains more than seventy species of poisonous plants, including datura, belladonna, foxglove—all our favorites.

There's also snakeroot, corn cockle, henbane, honeybush, cerbera odollam—which is apparently also known as the 'suicide tree'—yellow jessamine, and well, I won't keep reading. There are a lot of others—aha. Including hemlock. And they're adding to their collection all the time."

"Bingo."

Meredith read from the screen again. "The garden is open by guided tour only, and visitors are strictly forbidden to touch, smell, or taste the plants."

"I should say so."

"But on occasion, they have had visitors pass out because of the smell."

"Oh dear."

"'Many of the plants in the garden are often found in gardens around the world because people don't realize how dangerous they can be,'" Meredith read. "'We aim to educate visitors on the many ways plants can impact the human body, and also to raise awareness of the dangers lurking in everyday gardens.'"

"And no doubt they make a pretty penny on the visitors who come to see a poison garden."

"I'm sure they do. It does sound intriguing, doesn't it?" Meredith said.

"I'm not sure I'd say that."

"Look, here's a video with the current head gardener." Meredith clicked on the arrow to start the video. She quickly lowered the volume so she wouldn't disturb the other patrons, but no one seemed to notice. A jolly man in head-to-toe protective gear joyfully explained the toxicity of the plants in the garden. "This is atropa belladonna," he said, smiling. "Four of these berries will kill a child."

"He's a little too pleased about that," Julia said.

"The British accent makes it better somehow," Meredith said. Julia nodded.

"This plant is laurel, which is used to make cyanide. We all know what that can do to you," he said joyfully.

Meredith stopped the video. "Well, I officially want to go there now. They've somehow made something terrible look ridiculously interesting."

"Before you book your ticket, let's think about what this means," Julia said. "If he's the current head gardener, and he knows all about the toxicity of these poisonous plants, I think it's fair to assume that Elyse would also know about how toxic each of these plants was, since she was once the head gardener."

"I think you're right," Meredith said. "So. We know that Elyse was lying. Now we just need to figure out why."

Meredith started the video again, and they watched it until Maggie Lu came back. Meredith closed the video, and they both turned toward her.

She held out a thick, clothbound volume with yellowed pages and a tattered paper cover. *Secrets of the Medicine Woman*, the title read.

"This is the book." Maggie Lu held it out.

Julia took the book, opened the cover, and flipped through the pages. It was dense with small type and appeared to be organized by ailment—headache, stomach cramps, fever, and so on. Under each entry was a list of possible herbs and plants that could be used to treat it and how to prepare the treatment.

"There's an index where you can search by plant," Maggie Lu said.

Julia turned to the back of the book and found the entry for atropa belladonna. It was referenced in the sections for asthma, cold, hay fever, colic, diarrhea, and nerve pain. She turned to the entry for asthma and read how to boil the leaves and stems of the deadly plant to make a tea that would soothe bronchial spasms.

"Is there a warning about how the plant can also kill you?" Meredith asked.

"Maybe somewhere," Julia said. "But I don't see it here."

"Is there any way to know who checked this book out recently?" Meredith asked.

"I'm afraid we can't share that information," Maggie Lu said. "Because of privacy concerns."

Julia understood the reasoning, but it would have been so helpful if they could get that list of names. Still, maybe there was something she could learn in the book.

"Thank you," Julia said. "This is very helpful."

"It looks like we have some research to do," Meredith said.

Julia nodded. "Let's get started."

August 23, 1914

Dearest Eugenia,

I hope you're enjoying the Isle of Hope. I keep trying to convince Edward that we need a house there too, but he keeps putting me off because he has to work here in the city. I have told him his presence would not be required, but he does not seem to agree. I suppose he'll be sorry when I roast to death here at home some August.

Did you hear about Victoria Dupriest? I noticed at Hazel's summer soiree that she had been getting a little too cozy with that Abernathy boy, and lo and behold, Victoria has been sent "to visit relatives in Europe." She won't be back until next spring, Helen said. Well. That is some wonderful timing, if you ask me. I suppose she'll be kept wherever she has really been sent until she gets her shape back, and then they'll bring her home around the debutante circle and pretend no one knows what happened. I don't know how Helen can hold her head up.

Speaking of which... I spoke with Nellie Gordon the other day. I thought I might be able to talk some sense into her and get her to put an end to the nonsense that Daisy has been up to with those young girls, but Nellie defended Daisy. Can you believe it? She says that Daisy is modeling what she's doing on something she saw in England, and Nellie told me that Daisy is helping the girls. Helping them, by teaching them to sleep on the ground and cook food over fire like savages! I don't know how Nellie can stand it. I have always said there was something not right about that family.

Come back soon before I melt.

Yours,

Hattie

After Julia and Meredith picked up the kids from the library's children's area, they headed back to the office, but the children soon got restless, and Meredith decided to take them to a local splash park to cool off.

After they left, the office got quiet, but Julia felt a strange sense of disappointment. It took her a moment to realize that being around Kinsley and Kaden made her miss Kennedy and Madison. Well, there was something she could do about that. She picked up her phone and dialed Wyatt's number.

"Hey, Aunt Julia," Wyatt said. "How are you?"

"I'm all right. Just missing my girls. I wondered if you all wanted to come over Friday night. We could do a cookout, if you're up for it. Beau has been itching to make another batch of barbecue."

"That sounds awesome," Wyatt said. "Let me check in with Anna Beth, and I'll let you know as soon as I can."

"Great. I'll talk to you soon."

Julia turned back to her screen and tried to prioritize their new leads: They needed to find out why Elyse had lied; they needed to learn more about Theo's arrest for poisoning his girlfriend; they needed to learn more about Calvin Corliss; and they needed to review the footage from the doorbell cameras, which had already started to arrive in her inbox.

What she really wanted to do was go back to Elyse and confront her with what she knew and ask why Elyse had lied to her. But in her experience, showing up on someone's doorstep and calling them a liar didn't always produce the best results. She would need to figure out a better way to approach that. In the meantime, she decided to start reviewing the footage that the animal hospital had sent her. But the file was huge. While she was waiting for it to download, Carmen appeared in the doorway.

"Hola." She had a manila folder tucked under her arm. "Do you have a second?"

"Apparently I have about thirteen minutes," Julia said, glancing at the little timer that estimated the time for the file to download. "What's up?"

"You asked me to find records about Calvin Corliss's arrest for drunk driving," Carmen said. "I found the records."

"Wonderful." Julia hadn't had much momentum with the parks department employee who frequented the park when he shouldn't have. "Have a seat. What did you find?"

Carmen sat in the chair and opened the folder. "This is the accident report for the incident you were interested in." She lifted a set of stapled papers from the stack and set them on the desk. Julia looked down at the top sheet. The date, time, and location of the arrest were noted, as well as the license plates of both cars involved. She also read that Calvin's Breathalyzer reading had registered at 0.13 percent. That was well over the legal limit, and he would certainly have been impaired at that level. Calvin was reported to have been belligerent at the scene and was taken to the police station.

"He appeared in court the next day." Carmen pushed another paper across the desk. "He was charged with a misdemeanor and ordered to pay a hefty fine and released."

"Was this a one-off?" Julia knew that sadly, many drunk driving incidents were caused by people with a string of similar incidents.

"I couldn't find any other police records, so I believe this is his only DUI."

"That's good. Maybe it scared him straight."

"I did find his name in another court record, but it doesn't appear to be anything particularly interesting," Carmen said. "After his divorce, his ex-wife was awarded full custody of their two children and he petitioned to have shared custody."

"Was he successful?"

"He was denied," Carmen said. "His ex-wife cited that drunk driving arrest and also claimed he was abusive. She appears to have filed a restraining order against him."

"How awful." Julia was very familiar with family court cases, and it was always heartbreaking to have parents come in fighting over the kids as if they were one more asset to squabble over in a divorce. But if his ex was able to get a restraining order, it sounded like there might be some validity to her claims.

"That's all I could find on him." Carmen closed the folder. "Though I'm happy to keep looking if you need me to."

"No, that's great," Julia said. Carmen headed back to her desk, and Julia saw that the file still had almost eight minutes before it would be done downloading. She decided to use the time to try to find contact information for Calvin Corliss.

They had phone books from all the local towns and suburbs here in the office, and she checked the one that included Pooler, but there was no listing for Calvin Corliss. That wasn't that surprising, really; so few people had landlines these days. She googled him and poked around online, finally stumbling on a homeowner's association discussion board for a housing development in Pooler. She scanned the many entries, which were mostly complaints about noise and neighbors not mowing their lawns enough and leaving trash behind at the community pool. She was encouraged to see that most of the posts were signed with a person's first name and their address.

She did a search for the name Calvin on the message board and came across a discussion thread about fireworks. Some neighbors had apparently complained about residents setting off fireworks in their yards, and there was a heated debate about whether they should be banned by the HOA. Julia found Calvin's post, in which he argued that fireworks were legal in Georgia and therefore banning them in a person's own neighborhood was an infringement of their rights. The post was signed, *Calvin, 42 Briarpatch Lane.* Now she had an address. Should she drive past his house and check it out? Julia considered it for a moment but then decided that could wait. He was almost surely at work at the moment. For now, the video was almost done downloading, so she made herself a cup of coffee and then sat back down and clicked on the file.

The first thing Julia noticed about the footage was the strange, almost fish-eye angle. It was disorienting at first, but she soon got used to it and saw that the camera, which was mounted by the door of the animal hospital, gave a view of the porch and the yard, but also the street and park beyond. The background images were small but certainly visible. The camera was designed, she saw, to give the owners a view of whoever was at the door.

Julia started the video and noticed that the footage was from the past two weeks. She watched as customer after customer came to the porch, clutching cats in crates or with dogs on leashes. The footage cut from one to the other abruptly, and Julia realized that the camera didn't record nonstop; it was motion activated, which meant that she didn't have to sort through hours of footage where nothing happened. But, she discovered as she watched, it also meant that she didn't get a good view of what was going on in the background, across the street at the park, because the people walking into and out of the park didn't set off the motion-activated camera. It was only set to record activity at closer range.

Still, it was useful, Julia thought, as she watched people come and go from the vet's office. The light changed as afternoon turned to evening, and then the footage jumped to the next morning, when Dr. Preston showed up to unlock the front door. Julia kept her eyes focused on the background in each shot, watching for anything out of the ordinary at the edge of the park, looking for people who appeared on multiple days or who seemed strange for any reason. It was difficult, because the footage was so jumpy, the camera turning on and off as people came and left the clinic, and because the people in the background were so small, but she did see a woman who appeared to be jogging along the perimeter of the park in shots over three different days. Julia made a note of her—tall, hair in a ponytail, wearing different jogging shorts and tank top each day, headphones on. Julia hoped she looked half as good as this woman when she ran.

Julia went back to her email and clicked on the next video she had received, which was from the owner of the building that housed the hair salon. While it downloaded, she dug around on the SCAD website, trying to figure out who to contact about getting access to any security camera footage they had from buildings along the park. She eventually found a generic email address for the facilities department, and she sent an email asking to see the footage, but she was not hopeful.

The video still had five minutes left to download, so she pulled out the book by the medicine woman she'd checked out from the library. She flipped through the pages, not really sure what she was looking for. The text was dense but full of information. *Belladonna can be used to cure stomach upsets*, the text read. *Boil leaves with catnip for an hour and strain into cup. Drink while hot.* Julia was pretty sure she wouldn't be trying that anytime soon. As she flipped, a small paper slipped out and landed on the floor. It looked like a receipt. She bent over and picked it up, and saw that it was a check-out slip, much like the one she'd gotten when she'd checked the book out earlier today. This slip said the book had been checked out by Margo Richardson and had been due in March of this year.

Huh. Why had Margo Richardson taken the book out? Julia wondered. Could she have been looking into plants for the garden?

It was worth looking into, she decided. She sent Meredith an email with the name Margo Richardson, explaining how she'd found it. Then she saw that the hair salon security camera footage was ready, so she set the book and the slip aside for now, and when she opened the video, she saw that this camera had the same fish-eye lens as the other footage. But she also saw that this system was different because it recorded continually, not just when someone was at close range. That meant that she had two full weeks of footage, starting two weeks ago yesterday, to review. *This will take forever*, she thought. But it might prove more useful. The house was set on Gaston Street, so it gave a different angle than the animal clinic on Whitaker.

She set the video to run at four times the normal speed and paid attention to the people walking toward the park. She really wanted to make note of anyone who appeared over multiple days, as those plants in the garden were thriving and were most certainly tended regularly.

There was her runner again, Julia noted. She appeared to make four loops around the park on the first day of the footage. There were many other people who came and went but none who stood out to Julia on the first day. The light faded from the sky, and Julia was pleased to see that the camera automatically changed to night vision when it grew dark. Not many people walked along the edge of the park after about nine, but Julia was still able to see a few. Finally, the sun came back up, and the streets began to fill once more. There went the runner again, Julia noted, doing her laps dutifully. Julia would need to try to figure out who she was, but so far wasn't too concerned with her. It was a mile and a half around the perimeter of the park, and this jogger was appearing on screen about every twelve minutes, which meant she was keeping a fast enough pace that she wouldn't have had time to stop and tend to the garden during her loops. Besides, she wasn't carrying any gardening tools, and there was nowhere to hide them on her tight clothing. Julia wasn't writing her off, but she wasn't especially interested in her as a suspect at this point.

It would take forever to go through two weeks' worth of video at this pace. But when she tried speeding the footage up even more, she couldn't get a good look at the people in the shot. This might take several days, unfortunately.

The sun set and rose again, and Wednesday morning saw the same jogger. But on Wednesday afternoon, something caught Julia's eye. There was a young woman who looked familiar. She was average height, with what looked like medium-brownish hair, though it was hard to tell. She wore sunglasses and a floppy hat and had what looked like a tote bag draped over one shoulder. Julia had seen her before. There was a girl just like her in the doorbell cam footage. Julia hadn't necessarily thought the sunglasses and hat were odd, because it was summer, and protecting yourself from the sun just made sense. But this girl wore them again on Wednesday afternoon as well. Was she protecting herself from the sun, or was she trying to make sure she wasn't recognized? Julia couldn't tell. And the way she walked just seemed...purposeful somehow. Most of the people who went by were strolling, gazing up at the trees or gawking at the houses along the park, but this girl walked like she had a destination. None of it was suspicious in itself, but Julia would keep an eye on her.

Julia went back to the first video—the doorbell cam from the animal hospital—and scrolled through the footage until she found her. She appeared in the background of the animal hospital footage on Tuesday around four. And here she was again. Julia clicked back to the newer footage, which gave a clearer shot. She was wearing a SCAD T-shirt, Julia saw. Maybe a student. There had to be plenty of them around for the summer. Julia went back to Wednesday, took a screen shot of the girl, and then she let the footage run again. When the sun set on Wednesday she paused the video.

Julia sighed and leaned back, stretching her arms over her head. She glanced at the clock and saw that somehow it was already past five. Time to pack it in for the day. She'd watch more of the footage tomorrow. She forwarded both videos to Meredith, noting the girl in the hat and sunglasses and telling Meredith at what point on the video to find her, and then she gathered her things and turned off her computer. She said goodbye to Carmen, who was also packing to leave, and headed home.

Beau had spent the day fishing, and he was in the garage putting away his rods and supplies when Julia pulled up.

"Successful day?" she asked, walking from her car to the garage.

"Depends on what you mean by success," Beau said, giving her the same crooked grin that had stolen her heart so many years before. "Buddy and I solved the world's problems, so that has to count for something, right?"

Buddy and Beau could spend hours on the boat discussing and giving their opinions on any topic.

Julia laughed. "Did you catch anything?"

"Several large redfish. I was thinking I would fry one up for dinner tonight."

"Change the frying to grilling, and you have yourself a deal."

"You always try to ruin my fun." Beau pouted, but she knew he was joking. As a retired anesthesiologist, Beau knew the importance of eating healthfully, but he still enjoyed fried food and all kinds of other Southern treats. "All right then. Once I get this cleaned up, I'll start working on the fish."

"Sounds great." Julia hitched her bag up on her shoulder. "Is there time for me to get in a short jog before dinner?"

"Of course." Beau smiled. "Back at it, huh?"

"I'm hoping that I'll hate it less if I don't have to wake up before the sun."

"It's great that you're doing this," Beau said. "I mean, I wouldn't want to run myself—don't get me wrong—but it's great to see you push yourself. And I know how much it means to Cassie. I would be proud to sponsor you for a hundred dollars."

"That's very generous."

"The school only gets the money if you do the race, though." He winked at her.

Julia leaned in to plant a kiss on his cheek before heading into the house to change into her running clothes. Bunny meowed and rubbed up against her legs as she drank a glass of water, and then Julia walked out onto the porch and headed out.

Instead of running through the neighborhood as she had before, she got in her car and drove the short distance to Lake Mayer Park, a local park with tennis courts, basketball courts, a playground, and a lake. Julia knew there was a trail that went around the lake and had seen runners on it in the past. She'd always wondered what had possessed them to do something so strange, but today, she climbed out of her car, adjusted her shoelaces, and found herself among them. She made her way to the paved path that followed the outside edges of Lake Mayer, and set off. There were a lot of people out, enjoying the summer evening, she noticed. There appeared to be some kind of basketball tournament in progress on the courts, and there were many families at the picnic tables and using the grills.

As she moved past the island where the main park facilities were located, there was the lake on one side of the path and trees on the other, and it was quiet, with just the sound of the water lapping against the shore and the wind through the trees. She'd read that the path around the lake was about a mile and a half long. She looped around the lake and ended up right back where she'd started. She'd had to walk on and off, and her lungs were burning and her legs were aching, but she'd done it. She wasn't quite ready to try the loop a second time—she'd have to work up to that—but she'd made it.

Somehow, Julia thought as she climbed back into her car and pumped up the air-conditioning, that hadn't been as terrible as she'd expected. She wouldn't say she'd enjoyed it, but it hadn't been awful. That was progress, she supposed. Maybe, just maybe, she'd be able to do this 5K after all.

***

Julia had just gotten out of the shower when her phone rang, and she saw that it was Wyatt.

"Hi there."

"Hi, Aunt Julia. Anna Beth reminded me that we have a dinner with our small group Friday night. But we'd love to see you. Is there any chance we could do tomorrow instead?"

Julia was pretty sure she didn't have anything going on in the evenings this week. "That would be fine."

"Awesome. And, uh, one other thing."

"Yes?" Julia felt a sense of dread as she realized what was coming.

"Mom was over here earlier watching the kids for a bit, and Madison mentioned we were going to see you, and, well, Mom really wants to come too."

"Oh."

"I'm sorry, I know this puts you in an awkward spot, but is there any chance…"

"Yes." Julia didn't know what else to say. She couldn't exactly say no, could she? "That should be fine."

"Thank you. She'll be so glad to hear it."

"I'll see you tomorrow. Around six?"

"That sounds perfect."

Julia hung up. She'd still get to see the kids, but it wouldn't be what she'd imagined.

Chapter Seven

WHEN JULIA GOT TO THE office on Thursday morning, after a plodding run in the humid air and a cool shower, Meredith and the kids were already there.

"You're here early." Julia set down her bag and poured herself a cup of coffee, and then she went over to stand in the doorway of Meredith's office.

"Oh good. You're here." Meredith was smiling at her a little too broadly. Kinsley and Kaden were both looking down at iPads, headphones on. Kaden seemed to be watching some sort of science video, while Kinsley's screen showed some sort of princess-themed cartoon.

"What's going on?"

"We're going on a field trip." Meredith was already standing up. "We should get going soon if we're going to be on time."

"We're what?"

"You don't have any meetings this morning, do you? Carmen checked your calendar for me, and you didn't have anything there."

"No... I..." She tried to wrap her head around this. "Where are we going?"

"Columbia."

"Columbia, South Carolina?"

"Yes. Not Colombia, the country. The South Carolina state capital."

"That's more than two hours from here."

"That's why we need to get going. We have an appointment at eleven."

Julia took a sip of her coffee, hoping the caffeine would cause this to make more sense.

"What kind of appointment do we have?"

"I'll explain in the car. Come on. Grab your things. I'll drive." Meredith gestured for her to get her purse.

A few minutes later, they were all in Meredith's SUV, the kids glued to their screens in the back seat, and as Meredith threaded through the narrow streets of the historic district, she explained.

"I started out by watching some of those videos you sent."

"Did you see the girl in the SCAD shirt?"

"I did. And I think she's someone we need to look into, for sure, so I took a screenshot of her in the video and I have that on my phone. But after a while, I got frustrated watching a little gray screen for so long, so I also did some research into Margo Richardson."

Julia searched her memory for the name. "That's the person who checked out the book about the poisonous plants from the library?"

"Sharp as ever."

"I think I need more coffee. I can't see how any of this makes sense."

"Margo Richardson is a student at SCAD."

"Oh." Julia was beginning to understand. "But there are lots of SCAD students around."

Meredith slowed to let a man walking a dog cross the street, and then started again. The expressway was just ahead of them.

"But how many of them would have checked out a book that discusses the use of poisonous plants?"

Julia couldn't argue with that. But she had another question. "If she's in Savannah tending a garden, why are we driving to South Carolina to see her?"

"She has an internship in Columbia for the summer, so I know she's there now," Meredith said. "But it's not that far from Savannah. Maybe she goes back and forth between Columbia and Savannah."

"Huh?" Julia wasn't tracking.

"I mean, maybe she's from Columbia and returns to campus regularly. Or maybe she's just there for the summer, for her internship, and comes back to Savannah sometimes. Or maybe she's from Savannah and is spending the summer in Columbia."

"In other words, you don't know."

"That's why we're going to talk to her." Meredith shrugged. "It's not so far that she couldn't make the drive a few times a week if she had a good reason. Say a boyfriend, or a secret garden plot she had to tend."

"Are we seriously driving all the way to Columbia because this girl goes to SCAD, and there's also a girl on the footage we saw who is wearing a SCAD T-shirt?"

"No, we're driving all the way to Columbia because she checked out a book about cultivating and using poisonous plants, including the ones we found planted in the park. And I have a hunch she can help us."

"Okay." Julia still wasn't convinced this trip was totally necessary, but she was willing to go along with Meredith's hunches. They'd often proven right in the past.

"How did you arrange this so quickly?"

"I was looking her up after the kids went to bed, so I sent her a message. She responded right away." Meredith flipped on her blinker and pulled onto the expressway.

"What did you tell her when you asked to make an appointment?"

"I told her I was interested in her work." Meredith merged easily in the light traffic.

"What is her work, exactly?"

"Painting. She's a visual arts major. And her work really is lovely. She has a portfolio posted online, and I liked what I saw."

"So this poor girl thinks we're coming all this way to talk about buying her paintings?"

"She thinks we're going to talk to her about her paintings. And since I looked at her paintings online, I can do that. Why don't you look her up so you can discuss them with her too?"

Julia still wasn't sure about this, but they were already on their way now. She pulled her phone out of her purse and did a Google search for the name Margo Richardson. She found a sleekly designed website that showcased her paintings, which featured abstract swirls of color. They were a bit modern for Julia's taste, but she could see the appeal.

A pleasant silence fell over the car as they passed the exit for Hilton Head.

"So. How's the running going?" Meredith asked after a few minutes of quiet.

"Ugh."

"That good?"

"I'm so sore."

"You're raising money for what with this race?"

"A new air conditioner for the kids' school."

"That's a worthy cause. I'd be happy to sponsor you. Thanks for asking." Meredith grinned at her.

"You'd really sponsor me?"

"Of course. I want to support you and the school. Sign me up."

"Okay." Julia was strangely touched.

"Plus, this way I know you'll have to actually do it."

"Beau said the same thing."

"It turns out we both know you well."

Julia shook her head. "Why anyone chooses to run for fun is beyond me."

"I bet as you continue to work at it, it'll get easier."

"I hope so. So far, with every step, I just blame Cassie for doing this to me."

Meredith paused for a moment, and then said, "Tell me more about that."

"About what?"

"Cassie. Do you really resent her for it?"

"I mean, if I'm honest, yeah, kind of."

"She didn't force you into running the race, did she?"

"She didn't force me, no, but she pretty much guilted me into it."

"How did she do that?"

"She told me it's so important for the kids' school, what would the girls think if I quit now, this was something we could do together, and blah blah blah."

"She said it's something you could do together?"

"Yes, but I'm half expecting to show up the day of the race and have her not there because she forgot or because something better came up."

"Have you tried actually running with her?"

"No," Julia said grudgingly.

"Maybe it's worth a try. Don't shoot the messenger here, but I'm just trying to suggest that maybe she's genuinely trying to make a connection."

"If she is, then why couldn't she pick something I was actually interested in doing? This is all about her, just like everything always is."

Meredith was quiet for a moment before she said, "This isn't about running, is it?"

Julia didn't really have to think about her response. "No, it's not."

"Have you ever talked to Cassie about how you feel? Just get it all out there about how you felt hurt and abandoned and used, and how you're glad she's back but you're having a hard time trusting her?"

"Kind of." When Cassie had come to visit to help Mom, they'd talked about how Mom and Dad had loved Cassie and Julia equally, even though Cassie had never seemed to believe it. But Julia had never told Cassie why she didn't trust her to do what she said she would do. "We don't really talk like that in our family. We're better at burying our feelings. It's easier that way."

"And how is that working out for you?"

Meredith just didn't understand. She and Ron had had such a perfect marriage, such a loving and supportive family who all got along. It just wasn't like that for Julia, at least when it came to Cassie. "It wouldn't work. She's run away from every hard thing in her life for decades. She wouldn't just sit there and let me air my grievances. She'd never make it through the first bullet point."

Meredith was quiet again, for longer this time. Julia could tell by the look on her face that she was thinking something she wasn't sure she should say.

"What?" Julia finally asked.

Meredith pursed her lips, and then said, "Are you sure it's Cassie who's running away from something hard in this case?"

Julia ran the words back through her head and let them settle.

"You don't know what she's like," she finally said. "Even if I could get her to sit down long enough to talk about this, it wouldn't be this magical kumbaya moment like you're imagining. She's never been the kind to care about other people's feelings or take responsibility for her actions."

"Is there any chance she's changed over the years?"

"I doubt it."

"Something brought her home again after all this time."

"Yeah. She was finally out of money."

"That's not all it was."

Julia had to admit Meredith was right. Cassie had come home after their mother took a nasty fall. She'd said she was coming home to help care for her, and if Julia was honest, she had been doing that.

"Fine. She's helping with Mom."

"That shows growth of some kind, doesn't it?"

"I guess."

"I know you're wary. I know you've been hurt too many times by your sister. And I wouldn't presume to tell you what to do. But I am suggesting that it sounds like she's trying and maybe you could let yourself trust that she won't flake out on you this time. If she does, well, there's your answer. But if she doesn't—if she really is trying to find a way to connect again—then you've taken the first step toward healing that relationship."

Julia didn't know what to say. Maybe Meredith was right, in a way. But what happened if Cassie didn't come through this time? If Julia let herself trust her and then she was let down once again? Julia wasn't sure she could handle it.

"Resentment is easier," Meredith said. "And she's given you plenty of reason to resent her over the years. But if you want to bring healing to the relationship, you'll have to allow yourself to be vulnerable and to trust her a little bit."

Julia thought these words through. Did she want healing in the relationship? She supposed she hadn't really thought about it. She hadn't really considered it a possibility.

"I don't know."

"That's okay," Meredith said. "Just think about it."

Julia nodded. She wouldn't be able to not think about what Meredith had said. They sat in silence for a while, the tires smoothly eating up the miles, and then, from the backseat, Kinsley called out, "How much longer?"

Julia met Meredith's eye and smiled.

Meredith shook her head. "We'll be there soon."

The conversation moved to more neutral topics, and the rest of the drive passed quickly. Meredith followed the directions on her GPS to a modern redbrick building with a gleaming sculpture in front of it.

"What is this place?" Kaden asked, his tone skeptical.

"It's the Columbia Museum of Art," Meredith said as she drove around to the parking lot.

"Wait. We came all this way to go to a *museum*?" Kinsley's eyes were wide.

"Don't worry, I won't drag you through all of it. We're just here to talk to someone."

"Margo is here?" Julia realized she should have asked more questions.

"She's an intern here. She said to text when we got here and she'd bring us in."

Meredith parked the car, and Julia got out. It felt good to stretch her legs after the car ride. Meredith sent the text, and a moment later said, "She says to wait for her by the fountain in the plaza."

"Is that the metal thing?" Kinsley asked.

"I guess it must be," Meredith said. They all walked around to the front of the building and toward the gleaming swoops of metal that made up the fountain. Water trickled gently down from the top, gathering in a small pool beneath. Watching the water cascading down the metal entertained the children until a woman with bobbed dark hair stepped out of a door to the side of the main entrance and started walking toward them. She couldn't be much more than five feet tall. It wasn't the girl in the video footage, Julia saw that immediately.

Meredith waved. "You must be Margo."

She nodded. "Meredith?"

"It's great to meet you." Meredith shook Margo's hand and said, "This is my business partner Julia, and these are my grandkids, Kaden and Kinsley."

"It's nice to meet you all," Margo said. She had skin so pale it was almost translucent, and her thick eyeliner and dark lipstick somehow made her seem even younger than college age. "Let me get you inside, and then we can talk."

She led them back to the side door and used a keycard to unlock it, and then she ushered them all into the building.

"So you mentioned you're interning here this summer?" Meredith probed as Margo led them into a hallway lined with doors. Fluorescent lights gave the place a sickly yellow tinge.

"That's right. There's a special exhibit about Georgia O'Keeffe at the museum this summer, and I'm very lucky to be able to help with that. O'Keeffe is a big influence on my work, so it's pretty much a dream come true. I've studied every painting in depth and read every book that even mentions her work—like seriously, anything that's even related to what she painted. I've read about her, but I want to know all about her influences, you know? So I'm, like, a self-proclaimed O'Keeffe expert, and it's so great because my job is to stand around the exhibition gallery and I get to help answer any questions that the visitors have about her work. I'm on my lunch now, so I figured we'd talk in the break room, but would you like to see the gallery?"

"That would be wonderful," Meredith said, smiling.

"I would love that," Julia added. She didn't know a lot about fine art, but she had always found O'Keeffe's flowers quite pretty.

"Can we stay here and play video games?" Kinsley asked.

"No you may not," Meredith said. "You guys are about to see some work from one of the most famous American artists. Not every kid gets to see this stuff."

The looks on the kids' faces showed their displeasure, but they seemed to know better than to argue with their grandmother.

"It's really an interesting collection," Margo said as she led them out of the hallway through a door and into the public lobby area. The ceilings soared, and the wide-open atrium was sunny and bright. "Many people don't realize how O'Keeffe's time in South Carolina changed her painting."

People were milling around and sitting on stone benches, and Margo waved them right past the lobby and into a room with high ceilings and white walls.

"I didn't realize Georgia O'Keefe lived in South Carolina," Julia said. Everything she'd heard about the artist said she'd lived in New Mexico.

"She did, actually. Before she was famous, she was your typical starving artist, and she took a job teaching here in Columbia for four dollars a week."

"Oh wow," Meredith said.

"South Carolina has some of the most stunning natural beauty, and O'Keeffe would take long walks around the Conagree River." Margo was leading them into one of the side galleries, which was hung with art that looked pretty old, in Julia's amateur opinion. "Georgia was classically trained, having been educated at both the Art Institute of Chicago and the Art Students League of New York, but she was becoming aware of the modernist movement in Europe."

Margo led them into another room, this one filled with paintings that looked a bit newer.

"It was during this period in South Carolina that O'Keeffe realized that all of her work to this point had been copying the techniques she'd been taught," Margo continued. "But she realized that they didn't really express what she was feeling. So she sat down and decided to experiment. She dipped her charcoal pencils in water and began playing with the fluidity of line. These are the first examples of the stylized, flowing lines that her work is so known for."

"Fascinating," Meredith said. "I had no idea."

"Like I said, most people don't realize that it was her time here in South Carolina that made her work what it is. A friend saw the work she did while she was here and marched it right up to a gallery in New York, and that launched her career. She ended up marrying the gallerist to boot."

"That's handy," Julia said.

"This exhibition displays some of O'Keefe's most famous paintings, as well as some of the paper works she made when she was living here in Columbia."

Margo led them into another gallery. On the wall of this one was a big sign that said GEORGIA O'KEEFE: HER CAROLINA STORY.

"This exhibit was assembled with loans from other museums, and we're very lucky that they've been so generous. It's not often you see so many of her most important works in one place," Margo said.

"Wow," Meredith said as she walked into the gallery.

Julia saw that hanging on the walls at this end of the gallery were works on paper, mostly black and white, but Margo was right that in them you could see O'Keeffe playing with the movement of lines. And at the far end of the gallery were some paintings that Julia recognized. There were several up close views of flowers, as well as several that included cow skulls flying above desert scenery. Julia stopped and looked at one of a yellow flower. YELLOW CALLA, 1926 the plaque next to the painting read. ON LOAN FROM THE SMITHSONIAN MUSEUM OF AMERICAN ART. It depicted an up close view of the petals, with nuances of color as the petals moved in and out of shadow, and it was strikingly beautiful. Julia could almost smell the sweet, heady scent of a lily as she stood looking at it.

"Flower, flower, weird lines," Kaden said as he went along the galley. "Flower, cool, a skull! Flower, more weird lines."

"I like this one," Kinsley called, pointing at a large pink flower with a kind of rainbow on the side.

"That one is called *Hibiscus with Plumeria*," Margo explained. "She painted that one on a visit to Hawaii."

The collection really was incredible, and Julia realized how lucky they were to get to see it. But she was also starting to get antsy. They had come all this way. When were they going to question Margo about the book of poisonous plants?

She spotted Meredith at the far end of the gallery, looking at what Julia immediately recognized as a famous O'Keeffe painting. It showed a close-up view of a white flower with a blue background.

"That's lovely," Julia said, coming up beside Meredith.

Meredith nodded but didn't answer.

"What is it?" Julia asked.

Instead of answering, Meredith pointed at the plaque on the wall next to the painting.

JIMSONWEED.

Chapter Eight

"Jimsonweed," Meredith said.

Julia read the little plaque on the wall. Jimsonweed, 1932, On Loan from the Indianapolis Museum of Art.

"Jimsonweed," Julia said. "Otherwise known as datura, devil's trumpet, or thorn apple."

"This gives us a way to broach the subject," Meredith said. "And she's coming toward us now."

"This is one of O'Keeffe's most famous paintings," Margo said, coming up beside them. "It's called *Jimsonweed*, and the connection of that particular plant—at least using that name—to the South also makes it the centerpiece of this exhibition."

"It's wonderful," Julia said. "You mentioned that you read every book you could find that touched on O'Keeffe's subjects. Do you have an interest in plants beyond the paintings?"

"Not really." Margo shrugged. "I mean, sure, I like plants but I don't grow any or anything like that."

"I heard that Jimsonweed is poisonous," Meredith said. "Did you read anything about that in your research?"

"Oh sure," Margo said. "When I was researching this painting all the books mentioned that. I found all kinds of books about uses for Jimsonweed and how to make sure you don't have it in your garden and stuff like that. But I was only interested in the plant because of the painting."

"I see." Julia felt sure she was telling the truth.

"It's a delightful painting," Meredith said. "And when we looked you up online, we saw your gorgeous work," she added quickly. "And we really liked them. Now that I'm here, I can definitely see how your work is inspired by Georgia O'Keeffe. It has the same fluidity and nuance that hers has." Meredith smiled. "It's really incredible."

Margo's face softened, and her posture relaxed.

"Seeing this now, I like your work even more. In fact, I noticed that you had a small painting of a lily that reminded me in some ways of the red poppy painting over there," Meredith said.

Had there been a painting of a red poppy on Margo's site? Julia had missed that.

"I was inspired by O'Keeffe's work," Margo said. "For sure."

"Yet you bring your own style to it," Meredith said. "I saw the price you had listed on your site. It seems fair."

Margo brightened. Julia widened her eyes. Was Meredith really going to buy one of Margo's paintings?

"If I gave you a check today, could you mail the painting to me?" Meredith asked.

"Of course. I'd be happy to." Margo beamed.

"Wonderful." Meredith smiled again. "Now, I was wondering if you would be able to help us with one more thing. We are interested in talking to someone we think goes to SCAD." She pulled her phone out of her purse and opened the photos to the screenshot of the girl in the SCAD shirt from the doorbell footage. "Do you recognize this girl?"

Margo took the phone and used two fingers to enlarge the image. She pressed her lips together, and then she shook her head.

"She doesn't look familiar. I mostly hang out with other visual arts majors, and she's not one of us."

She squinted, pinched the image larger, and then smaller again. "It looks like she's wearing a SCAD Eco Club shirt."

"She is?" Julia leaned in. Where had it said that?

"See that thing there?"

Julia squinted. Margo was pointing at the small blob of some kind beneath the letters.

"That's their logo. It's a leaf holding a protest sign. It's kind of stupid, if you ask me. But that's what it is."

"How can you see that?" Julia couldn't see anything more than a blob.

"It's kind of hard to tell here, I'll admit, but you see the shirts around campus. It's the only thing like it."

"And would this person most likely be in the Eco Club?" Meredith asked.

"I would imagine. No one else would be wearing that shirt."

"What sorts of things does the Eco Club do?" Julia's mind was racing. Surely some of the members were into plants. Did it extend to flowers?

"Oh I don't know. I don't pay too much attention to them, really. Mostly they seem to organize protests about climate change and make sure the cafeteria isn't using plastic forks, things like that." She shrugged.

"Is there a way to get a list of the members of the club?" Meredith asked.

"I don't know," Margo said again. "I'm not sure where that would be. I think you'd probably need to contact the club to find that out. Or maybe their website would say?" She shrugged. "I'm sorry I can't tell you more."

"Oh, you've been incredibly helpful," Meredith said.

"We really appreciate your time." Julia heard a noise behind her and turned to see Kaden spinning in circles, while Kinsley was lying on the bench in the middle of the room, her head hanging off one end. "It looks like we'd better get these kids out of here."

Meredith pulled her checkbook out of her purse, wrote a check, and then handed it to Margo.

"Thank you," Margo said.

"I can't wait to hang it on my wall."

Margo waved and then turned to a patron who was waiting to ask a question. Meredith and Julia gathered the kids and led them outside and back to the car. Before leaving Columbia they stopped at a pizza restaurant with black vinyl booths and high ceilings and lots of marble and subway tile. The menu offered many gourmet varieties, like prosciutto and caramelized fig and grilled honey sriracha chicken, but they stuck with plain old pepperoni. While the kids devoured the pizza, Meredith and Julia discussed what they'd learned.

"It definitely wasn't Margo in the video," Julia said. "And after talking with her, I believe her reasons for looking at that medicine woman book."

"I do too, unfortunately," Meredith said. "But the tip about the Eco Club was really helpful. We'll have to find a way to research the members."

Julia nodded. "At least we learned that. The trip wasn't a total waste of time."

"Of course it wasn't. We learned about one of the most important American painters and saw some of her works. That's huge." Meredith took a sip of her sweet tea. "Sheri Lynn will be pleased that I exposed the kids to culture. She's always looking for ways to 'broaden their horizons.'" She said this last part with air quotes. "Plus, I got a painting."

"You didn't have to do that, you know," Julia said.

"I know I didn't. But I actually like it. I think it's pretty. And the colors will go well in my guest bathroom. Plus, it really didn't cost very much. And after she'd let us all into the museum for free, it was the least I could do."

"It was very generous."

"No it wasn't. I actually *like* the painting," Meredith insisted.

"All right." Julia was glad she did, and she would leave it at that. "So I guess we have our marching orders when we get back, right?"

"That's right. We start trying to figure out the list of members of the Eco Club." Meredith nodded. "And we confront Elyse about why she lied."

"Confront her?"

"Yes. We know she's lying. How else are we going to find out why?"

Julia thought about it for a moment and then said, "All right. Maybe we can pay her a visit on our way home."

Meredith nodded. "That sounds like an excellent idea to me."

***

Meredith let out a low whistle as they pulled up in front of Elyse's estate on the Isle of Hope. "Not a bad place."

"You should see the view from the back porch," Julia said, pushing open her door.

Meredith turned to the kids in the back of the SUV. "Come on. Time to go."

"Can't we just stay here?" Kaden asked without looking up from his screen.

Julia had been wondering that as well. How would they confront Elyse with two children in tow?

"Nope. You can get arrested for that kind of thing these days." Meredith gestured for them to get out. "When your dad was young, I would just leave him and Uncle Chase in the car while I went grocery shopping, but times have changed."

After some grumbling, the kids put down the iPads and followed Julia and Meredith to the front door. Julia rang the doorbell, and a few moments later, Elyse answered it.

"Oh. Julia. Hello." She took a step back. Her hair was in a high ponytail, and she was wearing tennis whites.

"Hi, Elyse. This is my business partner, Meredith, and her grandchildren, Kaden and Kinsley."

Elyse nodded uncertainly.

"We were wondering if we could talk to you for a moment."

"I—" She broke off and looked around. "I guess." But she didn't move to let them in.

"Thank you," Julia stepped forward, and Elyse moved out of the way, grudgingly leading them into a formal parlor. The walls were red, and the furniture was heavy and dark. An oil painting of a man in historic army dress hung over the carved marble fireplace.

Elyse indicated that they should sit on a high-backed wood-framed sofa upholstered in plush cream velvet, and the kids were directed to matching chairs on either side.

"A dog!" Kinsley said, pointing at the sheltie curled up by the fireplace.

"That's Charlie," Elyse said. "He's very friendly, if you want to pet him."

Kinsley was already on her way across the room when Julia said, "He also loves to play fetch." She turned to Elyse. "Would it be all right if they took him out to the yard to play?"

"That would be wonderful," Elyse said. "He would certainly appreciate it."

"Yes!" Kinsley said.

"I'll show you the yard," Elyse said. Then she added, "Come on, Charlie." The dog hopped up right away and followed Elyse outside, Kaden and Kinsley following behind.

"This place is incredible," Meredith said as soon as Elyse was out of earshot. She touched a cut-glass candy dish on the mahogany side table next to the couch. "It's like a museum."

"She loves antiques." It was a bit fussy for Julia's taste, but she had to admit it was beautiful.

"She wasn't happy to see us," Meredith said.

"In her defense, she wasn't exactly expecting two grandmas and two children to show up on her doorstep uninvited," Julia said. The wooden arched back pressed into her shoulder, and she adjusted her position, trying to get comfortable. The old furniture might be lovely, but it wasn't especially comfortable.

Julia heard footsteps, and Elyse came back into the room. She took a seat on the wingback chair and smiled nervously at them.

"I'm sorry to drop in like this," Julia said. "But after talking with you earlier this week, we stumbled on something that left me confused."

"Oh?" Elyse was sitting still, her legs crossed at the ankle primly in front of her.

"We found an article about the Alnwyck Poison Garden," Meredith said. "And you were cited as the head gardener."

"You told me you were a gardener, but you neglected to mention that you were in charge of a poisonous garden," Julia said. "In fact, you told me that you didn't know anything about hemlock. But the website said it was grown in the poison garden."

Elyse pressed her lips together, her eyes darting from Julia to Meredith and back again.

"We were wondering why you lied," Meredith said gently.

Elyse sat in silence for a moment and then let out a breath.

"Okay. Obviously I didn't tell you the truth about my knowledge of toxic plants, and I'm sorry about that. But I didn't plant those flowers in Forsyth Park, I swear to you. I almost never go downtown, and I would never put those plants in a public garden. I know, better than most, how dangerous they can be. Whenever I went into Alnwyck Poison Garden, I went in protective gear. You can't mess around with toxic plants, believe me. They can kill people and animals. Besides—" She gestured at Julia. "You saw my garden. If I wanted to plant poisonous plants, why wouldn't I just do it here?"

"Maybe you didn't want Charlie to get into them?" Meredith suggested.

Elyse narrowed her eyes. "What, and expose other people's dogs?" She shook her head. "I may not have told you the whole truth about this one thing, but I'm not a monster. I would never put other people's pets at risk."

The way she said it, Julia actually believed her. She seemed totally disgusted by the idea.

"If that's true, why didn't you just tell me that?" Julia asked. "Why did you say you didn't know anything about poisonous plants?"

Elyse hesitated again for a moment before she said softly, "Because you're a PI."

Julia ran that around in her head, trying to make sense of it.

"What?" Meredith asked. "Why wouldn't you tell us the truth because of that?"

Elyse pressed her lips together again, looking down at the ground, and then she seemed to make a decision. "Because I don't want you to arrest me," she finally said. "I'm sorry, it's true that I lied, but it's because I was scared."

"You didn't want us to arrest you?" Julia repeated. Did Elyse think private investigators were a branch of the police? Was she that confused about how things worked here?

"For what?" Meredith asked.

Again Elyse hesitated, but then she said, "Because of the parking tickets."

"What?" Now Julia was really confused.

"I don't go downtown much now, but I used to, when we first moved here," Elyse said. "I loved walking around the quaint little squares and popping into shops. It's such a beautiful city. But I didn't really understand the parking situation."

"Ah, yes," Meredith said. "You mean the absence of parking situation."

The historic district was built well before the advent of cars, and its narrow streets that snaked around the historic squares were notoriously frustrating for driving and nearly impossible for parking.

"I acquired nearly half a dozen tickets in the first few months," Elyse said. "But I didn't—"

She broke off and composed herself before starting again. "I couldn't tell Bryce. He was so stressed already, with the new job, and I didn't... Well, he doesn't check my spending, exactly, but he does look at the bills every once in a while."

Now that she had decided to tell them what was going on, the words didn't stop.

"He'd been so nervous about me driving here, you see. I didn't drive at all while we lived in Chicago, because I didn't need to, so this was my first real opportunity to drive here in the States, and you all drive on the wrong side of the road, so Bryce was worried, but I promised him I'd be fine. And then I went and ran up all those parking tickets, and I just couldn't tell him. And I figured, if I ignore them, what are they going to do to me?"

"So you just didn't pay them?" Meredith asked, her eyebrow cocked.

"I know, it's silly. It seemed like such a small thing at first. Bryce, he's just... He's always so stressed, and I didn't want to upset him. He lets me do what I want, as long as it doesn't cause him any stress, you see?"

Julia was developing a pretty good picture of Bryce. She guessed him to be controlling, with anger issues. But she reminded herself she didn't know him and was only hearing one side of the story.

"And I figured, it's a *parking ticket*. What are they going to do, come after me for a parking ticket? I got a few back home in the UK, and I would just ignore them until they went away."

Julia wasn't sure what kind of financial system the local government there used that the money owed to the city would just be forgotten. It didn't work that way in Savannah.

"Did the city of Savannah follow up on the tickets?" Meredith asked.

"I got several notices in the mail, which I just threw right into the garbage. But then I got one that looked different. It was a notice to appear in court."

Julia knew it could get worse than that. If the unpaid parking tickets continued unpaid, the court could issue a warrant for Margo's arrest.

"That's when I started to get worried. I did some research online, and that was a mistake. The internet had me convinced that a member of some secret police force would show up at my door and take me to some underground detention center and hold me without contact with the outside world. Which I guess sounds silly, but I was scared."

"The internet is a scary place," Meredith said, nodding. "Never try to diagnose an illness online. You'll end up convinced you're on your deathbed."

"Tell me about it." Elyse adjusted in her seat and let out a breath. "That was Monday night. And then Tuesday you show up"—she smiled ruefully at Julia—"asking me about those plants, and I thought... Well, I know it sounds silly, but I just wasn't sure. I mean, I knew you weren't going to arrest me for my parking tickets when you were asking about flowers. Even I'm not that out of touch. But I'd read that if you have any legal trouble in your file, it can count against you when you show up in court, and I wasn't exactly sure how much influence PI's have. If I admitted my knowledge of poisonous plants, would you have told the police I was behind the plantings, and would that affect what happened when I appear in court? It seemed better just to...deflect the questions."

Deflect. A creative way to say lie.

"I'm sorry I wasn't honest with you. You guys probably think I'm a nutter. Please believe me when I say I don't make a habit of lying. I was just scared and not sure how it all works, and... Well, I'm sure it all sounds very silly."

"We know it can be challenging to be in a new place and not understand how things work," Julia said.

"Thank you," Elyse said. "And I know my word probably doesn't count for much right now, but I really don't know a thing about the plants in Forsyth Park. I wish I did—I would like to give whoever planted them a talking-to. Someone could get very seriously hurt. But it wasn't me."

This time, Julia believed her. They could cross one suspect off their list. But they were still no closer to solving the mystery.

Chapter Nine

WHEN THEY GOT BACK TO the office, Meredith took the kids to her house. Her younger son Chase was coming to spend the weekend with her and the kids, and Meredith wanted to get his room ready before he arrived. Julia went to her office to organize her thoughts. Elyse was off the suspect list, as was Margo, but they still had to find out more about Theo Williams and what happened when his girlfriend was poisoned. Then there was Calvin Corliss, the parks worker who had been spotted in Forsyth Park even though he shouldn't have been there. And there was the lead of the girl in the SCAD Eco Club T-shirt. And Julia still had to finish watching the footage from that security camera at the hair salon.

She decided to start by trying to get ahold of the parks department security camera footage. She called Randy Torrez, hoping for an update.

"Hi there, Ms. Foley. Have you had any luck finding who planted that garden?" Randy asked.

"Not yet, I'm afraid," Julia said. "How about the police? Have they found anything yet?"

Randy laughed. "They finally came to look at the area yesterday, but they didn't seem too concerned with it."

Julia wasn't surprised, though she wished she were.

"Are you able to remove the plants now?"

"Not yet. We're still waiting for a report from one of our plant specialists that will detail the safety precautions needed to protect the workers who do it."

Julia wondered how long that could possibly take.

"Is there any chance you were able to get security camera footage from the area?" she asked.

Randy let out a sigh. "We're supposed to get some this afternoon. Why it's taking so long is beyond me. The bureaucracy in this place is shocking. But I'm told it'll be coming. I've also been warned that the camera closest to the garden was broken."

"Really?" Had the person who planted the garden been behind that?

"Not smashed or anything exciting like that, though," Randy said. "Just gave up the ghost, and they hadn't gotten around to replacing it yet. Because, bureaucracy."

"That's frustrating."

"Tell me about it. But I'll let you know when I get the footage in."

Julia thanked him and hung up, and then she decided to focus on trying to find the Eco Club girl. She dug around on the website for the Savannah College of Art and Design and found a phone number for the dean of student life, who, from what she could tell, would be in charge of the clubs and activities on campus. Julia guessed that if anyone could give the name of the students in the club, the dean could, but when she called she got a voice mail. She left a message, not optimistic about the chance of a return call.

Next she tried to find out more about the Eco Club itself. A bit of googling turned up a few results, including the club's website, which gave some very basic information about the club and what they did. It also featured the logo of the leaf holding a protest sign, just as Margo had said, and now that Julia saw it herself, she could see how the blob on the girl's shirt could be this logo. The page was obviously not updated very often, as the Upcoming Events section listed an Earth Day Vigil from more than a year ago.

Julia clicked back to the search page and found a story in the student newspaper about a climate change march the Eco Club had participated in. Nicola Fabens, the president of the club, had been quoted in the article as saying, "This is a problem that we are determined to help fix. Today, we are uniting with people from all over the globe to tell our leaders that change is needed and that we won't rest until we see it happen." Julia used the SCAD email format to send Nicola a message, but she had no idea whether it would go through or whether she would get an answer.

Julia didn't find anything else about the club online. Well, if she couldn't find what she needed online, she would just have to go ahead and find it out in person.

She opened up a search window and studied a map of Savannah College of Art and Design. It was a sprawling campus, with build-ings located all throughout the city. She did some digging on the website and saw that the executive and administrative offices were located in Lai Wa Hall, directly across the park on Drayton Street. Julia pushed herself up, grabbed her purse, and walked around her desk into the hallway.

"Headed out?" Carmen asked, looking up as Julia walked into the lobby.

"Yes, I'm going to go try to talk to someone at SCAD," Julia said. "I don't know how long I'll be."

"No problem. We got a few calls from potential clients asking about fees, but I'll take care of those. Good luck."

"Thank you."

Julia walked out into the steamy air and crossed the street. SCAD was on the far side of the park, so she figured she'd cut through it. It was cloudy this morning, but there were still plenty of people out strolling and posing for selfies in front of the fountain. She heard the happy shouts of children coming from the playground as she walked. She decided to peek at the garden again, to see what shape it was in, but when she made her way through the azaleas, she saw that not only were the plants still there, but the caution tape had been ripped off and balled up and left nearby. She looked closer, and she saw that several stems had been snipped and several flowers removed. Had whoever planted them come back and been upset to find that their secret garden had been found? Or what if someone stumbled back here and didn't realize the plants were indeed poisonous? She picked up the ball of caution tape and did her best to unravel it and arrange it around the plants again, though it looked quite a mess. Still, it was better than having nothing there, she decided. Then she went back out to the main path and made her way out of the park and across the street to Lai Wa Hall.

Lai Wa Hall was a white-clad beaux arts building, with Palladian windows and Ionic columns flanking the entrance. Julia walked up the steps and into the cool marble foyer, where she studied a sign that listed the offices. The dean of student life had an office on the second floor, she saw, so she crossed the inlaid wood floor and went up the cast-iron stairs. The floors creaked as she made her way down the hallway toward room 221. The door was open to a small office. A young woman with dark hair streaked with hot pink was looking at the computer screen. That could not be the dean.

"Excuse me?" Julia said.

The girl looked up and smiled. "Hi. Can I help you?"

"My name is Julia Foley. I was hoping to speak with the dean of student life." Now that she was inside, she saw that there was a door to the left. The dean's office must be behind that.

"I'm afraid she's on vacation this week. But I can pass along a message?"

"Well..." Julia thought about how to phrase her request. "I was hoping I would be able to find a list of students who are involved in certain activities around campus."

"Oh, I'm afraid we don't keep a list like that," the receptionist said. "Each club and sport has their own list, I'm sure, but there isn't, like, a centralized list that the dean keeps."

"Oh." Julia had known it was unlikely she would be able to see such a list, but it was disappointing to find that it didn't even exist.

"But maybe I can help. I'm Lynley. What specifically were you looking for, Mrs. Foley?"

"I was hoping to find the names of the students in the Eco Club." Julia pulled her phone out and scrolled to the photo of the girl in the SCAD eco shirt and then held it out. "Do you by chance know who this is?"

Lynley narrowed her eyes and looked down at the phone. "I don't know her. Who is she?"

"That's what I'm trying to find out. I think she's in the Eco Club because of the logo on her shirt."

"Yep, that's it all right. It's a safe bet she's in the club. But I don't know who she is."

"Would you happen to know anyone in the club?"

"Yeah. My old freshman year roommate Heather is in it. She's great, but our room always smelled like patchouli."

"Is there any way Heather would be able to help me?"

"Maybe." Lynley shrugged. "I can text her and find out. Why?"

Julia weighed how much to say. "I'm interested in finding someone who's around for the summer and knows a lot about plants."

"They sure do talk a lot about plant-based diets, so they might know. I'll see if Heather can help."

"Is there any chance Heather is on campus for the summer?" Julia asked.

"Nah, she's got an internship in Atlanta."

"Is there any way to get a list of the students who are on campus for the summer?"

"I know the answer to that one. Not a chance, I'm afraid. Privacy violation and all that."

Julia nodded. That made sense.

"But I can tell you that most students get as far from this place as they can during the summer."

"But you're here."

"I'm working on my senior project, so I need access to the school's equipment."

"What is your senior project?"

"I'm a film major, and I'm working on a short piece about the growing problem of homelessness in the city. Profiling a few people recently pushed out by gentrification, that kind of thing."

"Wow. That sounds very serious."

"I'm trying to make a difference, you know?"

Julia nodded. It was nice to see a young person interested in helping people.

"But I need to use the school's equipment because I can't afford cameras like that myself. So here I am. I work here during the week and work on my film on the weekends."

"That sounds grueling."

"It's not so bad." She shrugged. "Dean Whitmer is pretty cool, and the job isn't exactly hard, you know? There's not a lot going on during the summer."

"Well, I really appreciate your help." Julia left a business card so Lynley could contact her if Heather was able to provide some names, and headed back to the office. She didn't hold out a lot of hope that Heather would come through, or, even if she did, that the names would be of much use. She could only hope there would be a break-through soon.

When Julia got back to the office, she continued watching the video footage.

She picked up where she'd left off, with Wednesday night. Traffic outside the park slowed at night, but she still watched, and she saw the park lighten as the sun rose on Thursday. There were a lot of tourists walking around by Thursday midmorning, recognizable by their slow pace and their awed expressions as they gazed at the buildings that lined the park. They *were* quite stunning, Julia had to admit. But Julia watched, trying to notice the people who showed up on the footage, just as she had when they'd noticed the student in the SCAD shirt. By Friday afternoon, the people in the shot were all starting to blur together until, right around one thirty, Julia saw something familiar on the screen.

She backed the footage up and slowed it down, and sure enough, there was a man in a dark polo, just like the kind the parks department employees wore. He also wore sunglasses and a baseball cap, and…

Now that was interesting. She paused the footage and zoomed in.

That was it. This was their answer. The garden was planted and maintained by Calvin Corliss. The evidence was right there in front of her.

Chapter Ten

JULIA WATCHED THE FOOTAGE A few more times, just to make sure, and then let it run for a little while, waiting to see if the man appeared back on the screen again. He did, about a half hour later—and this time the camera got a better shot of him. She was sure it was him. She called Meredith, who picked up on the third ring.

"It's Calvin Corliss. He's the one who planted the garden."

"Hold on," Meredith said. Julia heard the sound of a lightsaber in the background, and it grew quieter as Meredith no doubt walked out of the room. "Okay. Now, what was that?"

"I'm looking at the footage from the security camera we got from a house across the street from the park. It's in your email."

"Okay," Meredith said. "And you saw Calvin?"

"Yes. It shows him walking along the northern edge of the park not last Friday but the Friday before. He's all covered up in a hat and sunglasses."

"Then how do you know it's him?"

"Because a half hour later, he walks back with his hat off, and you can see it's him. I looked at that photo I found of him online and compared it to the image in the video, and it's unmistakable."

"Okay," Meredith said, infuriatingly calmly. Why wasn't she as excited as Julia was? "So what makes you think Calvin is the one who planted the garden?"

"First, there's the fact that he's supposed to be at work at some other park, but here he comes in the middle of the day, walking along the north side of the park, right by where the poisonous garden was, like a man on a mission."

"What makes you think that?"

"He just…" Julia didn't know how to describe it. "Watch the video. You'll see. He just looks like he's got a purpose, and no one is going to distract him from it. Then, there's the fact that he's covering up so no one can see his face."

"It's not all that unusual to wear a hat and sunglasses in June."

"Right. He might be trying to avoid detection, or he might be trying to protect himself from the sun. But here's the kicker: he's also wearing a gardener's tool belt."

"What?"

"You know, it ties around your waist and has pockets for trowels, hand rake, pruning shears, that kind of thing. He has all those tools in his belt as he walks directly toward the hidden garden and returns a half hour later—about the amount of time it would take to tend a garden like that, right?"

"Well, that's interesting."

"It's him. It has to be him."

"Let me check out the footage myself. I'll call you back in a bit."

"Okay. But hurry."

"I will."

While Julia waited for Meredith to watch the video, she let the footage run on her end and saw him again, wearing much the same outfit and tool belt, the next Monday afternoon around the same time. He must have come to the park several times a week to tend to the garden.

Where was Meredith? Why wasn't she calling back? Julia could feel adrenaline rushing through her, just like she always did when she was on the verge of solving a case. While she waited, she kept the video streaming, trying to notice anyone else who seemed odd or appeared more than once, but she didn't notice anything. She thought she saw the girl who had been wearing the SCAD T-shirt again, but it was hard to tell. The runner showed up again, looping around the park every morning like clockwork. Julia wished she could run like that, but, well, not in this lifetime.

Finally, Meredith called back. "It's him, see?" Julia said.

"It does seem like we should talk with him."

"I have his address."

"You're going to go talk to him? Today?"

"I thought I might."

"Oh man. When?"

"After work, probably."

"I want to go with you. But I don't think I can get the kids out again today, unfortunately. They're way too into this movie, and Chase will be here soon. Plus, I promised them Eyeball Soup for dinner."

"Eyeball Soup?"

"It's just meatballs in sauce, but they decided the meatballs look like eyeballs, so, well…kids. The name stuck."

"It sounds delicious once you get past the name." Julia's stomach grumbled, and she suddenly realized it was nearly time to head home.

"I'm sorry that it means I can't go with you to Calvin's house."

"That's okay."

"Are you sure? Do you feel comfortable going on your own?"

"I'll be fine." Julia wasn't worried. "I'll stop in on my way home."

"All right then. Please be careful."

"I always am."

"And let me know how it goes."

"Will do."

Julia went back to watching the video footage run, and a few minutes later an email came in from her friend in the Bibb County Courthouse.

> *Hi, Julia, it turns out some of the records from the case you're looking into are sealed because the defendant was a minor, but here is what I was able to find. Please let me know if you need anything else.*
>
> *Barbara*

Julia clicked on the email. Her friend Barbara had come through, saving weeks of waiting for an FOIA request to work its way through the proper channels.

Julia opened the first file, which showed that Theo pled guilty to the charge of possession of an illegal substance with intention to distribute and poisoning not resulting in death. The actual terms of the plea deal were not supplied, and since the case had never gone to court, there were no court records.

She clicked on the next file, which was a police report. She read the officer's narrative, trying to make sense of the timing. Courtney had been sent to the hospital on March 19th, Julia knew. This police report had been filed the following day, when officers came to Theo's house to interview him about what had happened.

We arrived at the house and found Williams at home. He at first refused us entry, but then a woman, who identified herself as Williams's grandmother, came to the door and insisted he let us in. Mrs. Williams was quite elderly, and we learned throughout the course of our meeting that she does not see or smell well.

Theodore Williams was visibly nervous. We told him we were there to interview him about what had happened to Ms. Sosby, and he insisted that it was an accident. We asked to see his room, where the incident occurred, and the smell of marijuana was evident before we got inside the bedroom. A worktable along one wall was filled with plants under hanging lights, but we did not see any marijuana. Upon searching the premises, we found the plants hidden in a shed in the backyard. Mrs. Williams appeared to be surprised and claimed she did not know Williams was growing marijuana. We handcuffed Williams and brought him to the station and booked him for illegal possession with intent to sell and questioned him about the marijuana and the poisoned girlfriend.

It was signed by an Officer M. Hartson. Julia read it through twice, trying to picture it all. The comment about Theo's grandmother not seeing or smelling well seemed odd, but she supposed it was in reference to the fact that she had somehow not noticed that her grandson was growing an immediately identifiable and also pungent plant in her home. In any case, she didn't appear to have been suspected of any wrongdoing, because only Theo was brought to the station.

The next file attached to the email was a transcript of the interview the police had conducted with Theo at the station.

Hartson: This is Officer Michael Hartson, along with Officer Judy Chen, on March 20, interviewing suspect Theodore Williams. Theodore, can you please confirm that you have been cautioned and you have accepted legal representation from the state and your lawyer is present.

Williams: That's all correct, sir.

Hartson: Thank you, Mr. Williams. Now, can you please tell about the incident at your house yesterday?

Williams: Yes, sir. I was working on my science fair project, but my girlfriend, she came over and she was trying to get me to go to a party at [redacted]'s house. A bunch of kids from our school was going to be there, and [redacted] was bringing beer, and she wanted to go, but I told her I had to wait for my assays.

Chen: For your what?

Williams: For my project, I'm testing the absorption of herbivorous toxins. At that particular time, I was running an assay to test the concentration of atropine in the leaves of datura stramonium.

[inaudible]

Hartson: Okay, so you were doing schoolwork.

Williams: Sure.

Chen: You said you were testing the absorption of toxins. Absorption into what?

Williams: Skin, ma'am.

Hartson: What, human skin?

Williams: No, sir. Mice.

Chen: You were poisoning mice? How—

Williams: Only a little bit.

Hartson: Why—

Chen: This was in your bedroom? That's so [redacted].

Schoenwald: My client will not be answering any more questions about the nature of his school project.

[silence]

Chen: Okay. So you were working on your project. You would rather do that than go out with your girlfriend? See friends?

Williams: It's not that I didn't want to go. I did. But I had to finish what I was working on. You can't really mess with the timing when you're working with—

Schoenwald: He preferred to stay in.

Hartson: So, you wanted to stay in, your girlfriend wanted to go out. When did you give her the berries?

Schoenwald: You don't have to answer that.

Williams: I didn't give her the berries. In fact, I've told her at least a dozen times never to touch the leaves of atropa belladonna. But she was gettin' mad, trying to get me to go out, and I was gettin' mad because I told her to just go without me.

Hartson: You wanted her to be gone.

Williams: Not like that. I wanted her to go out if she wanted to, and yeah, I mean, it was hard to concentrate with her messing around while I was trying to work. So I told her to just go, and she got madder, and I guess, well, I guess I kind of told her that maybe we shouldn't be together anymore if she was going to hold me back.

Chen: How did she take that?

Williams: Not well, ma'am.

Chen: What was your relationship with Ms. Sosby like before this?

Williams: Good. Great. I mean, at first I couldn't believe someone like her was even interested in someone like me, but—

Hartson: Meaning what?

Williams: She's so... Well, she's real pretty, sir. [inaudible] And she's from the popular crowd, if you know what I mean. But she started calling, and then she started hanging around my house, and then we were dating.

Hartson: So she pursued you?

Williams: I would never have dared to ask her out. I would have been afraid she would laugh in my face.

Hartson: Do you know why she was dating you?

Williams: Sir?

Schoenwald: Please rephrase your question.

Chen: I think what he means is, did she know about all of the plants you had growing in your room when you started dating?

Schoenwald: *Don't answer that.*

[inaudible]

Hartson: *You said yourself you couldn't believe a girl like her would want to go out with a guy like you. Did it ever occur to you that she might have had a motive?*

Schoenwald: *Let's please focus on the events at hand. I don't see what this has to do with the events of last night.*

Chen: *All right. So after you told Ms. Sosby you wanted to break up with her, what happened?*

Williams: *Then she started gettin' hysterical, shouting so loud even my granny could hear.*

Hartson: *That's your grandmother, who we met at your house?*

Williams: *That's right. She's raised me since I was a kid.*

Hartson: *Where are your parents?*

Williams: *Both my parents died when I was a kid. So I live with my granny, but she doesn't hear very well. But Courtney was screamin' so loud, here she comes down the hall to see what was goin' on. And Courtney, she—I don't know what came over her, but she was yellin' about how dare I break up with her, I should be grateful someone like her would even want to date someone like me, all that.*

Hartson: *Did that seem like a logical reaction?*

Williams: *I've never broken up with a girl before, sir. I couldn't say.*

Hartson: *What I mean is, do you think she realized that you were about to cut off her access—*

Schoenwald: We can't speculate about the reasoning behind Ms. Sosby's hysterics. Let's focus on the facts.

Hartson: Fine. So what happened then?

Williams: And then she reaches out for my plants and starts knocking them over. I told her to stop, but she didn't. She knocked more over and I told her again to stop, those plants are important. So she says, "Yeah, I know, these plants are always so much more important than anyone." I told her that's not fair, it's not the same. So she plucks a bunch of berries off the atropa belladonna and says, "Tell me I'm more important to you than these plants."

Chen: What did you say?

Williams: I didn't say anything. I was so stunned, I didn't know what to say. So then, before I knew what was happening, she popped them in her mouth.

Hartson: How did you respond to that?

Williams: I told her she was crazy and to spit them out right away. Those things can kill you. She just sat there chewing them. So I went to her to try to get her to spit them out, and she started swinging her arms at me, telling me to get away.

Chen: How many berries would you say she swallowed?

Williams: Half a dozen maybe. I wasn't real sure.

Chen: How dangerous is that?

Williams: That's more than enough to kill a child. For a grown woman? It was going to make her real sick, at best.

Hartson: And what happened once she'd swallowed them?

Williams: She just kept screamin' at me.

[silence]

Williams: It's not like you see in the movies. She wasn't just going to drop dead on the spot. The poison works more slowly than that. I knew at first she would have dilated pupils and be sensitive to light, but that can lead to headache and rash, and dryness of mouth and slurred speech. Then you get into hallucinations, convulsions, and organ failure. But all of that takes time.

Schoenwald: In answer to your question, my client called 911 immediately.

Williams: That's right. I knew she needed medical treatment right away, so I called 911. She started yelling that she didn't want any doctors, and she was still screaming at me and tossing my plants on the ground when the paramedics arrived.

Hartson: She refused to go with them, it says.

Williams: She was outta her mind. I tried to get her to go, but she wouldn't do it. She just drove on home like nothin' was wrong.

Chen: Ms. Sosby did eventually go to the hospital, later that night.

Williams: That's right but not until she started vomiting, late. I called her and texted her all evening, begging her to go get medical help. But she wouldn't. Finally, her dad drove her in the middle of the night. She's texting me on the way, saying she's so sorry, she didn't mean to wreck my plants, and I'm like, girl, you need to get your stomach pumped right away. That was the last I heard from her, though I kept texting her all night. The next day, she texts me from the hospital to say her dad called the cops, and you guys showed up at my door sayin' I poisoned her. I didn't poison anyone. She knew they were poison, and she went and ate them anyway.

Hartson: Let's talk for a minute about that text Ms. Sosby sent you. You say she warned you that the police would be coming to talk with you?

Williams: Yeah, she told me her dad was sayin' I made her eat those berries, and he wanted to have me arrested for attempted murder. I told her he was—

Schoenwald: My client was surprised by Mr. Sosby's take on the events.

Hartson: But in the time between that text and our arrival in your home this afternoon, did you remove anything from your room?

Schoenwald: You don't have to answer that.

Williams: No comment.

Hartson: There were three large marijuana plants found hidden in the garden shed in the backyard. Your bedroom, where your other plants were, smelled strongly of marijuana.

[silence]

Hartson: Mr. Williams, were you also growing marijuana in your bedroom?

[silence]

Williams: I wasn't using it or selling it. I was just interested in the chemical structure of—

Schoenwald: My client is done answering questions at this time.

Julia read through the transcript twice, trying to make sense of all of it. Was Theo's account true? It certainly painted a different picture of the incident than what she'd gotten from the article in the paper. If he was right, it did seem like maybe the poisoning wasn't his fault, though the possession charge was valid. The problem was, there was no real way to know. She would have to keep looking.

The next file was a transcript of the 911 call Theo had made.

Operator: 911, what's your emergency?

Williams: We need an ambulance, quick. My girlfriend, she, oh man, she just swallowed some poisonous berries.

Operator: What is your location?

Williams: 674 Ridgewood Avenue.

Operator: An ambulance is on the way. What kind of berries did she swallow?

Williams: They were atropa belladonna.

Operator: And what is her condition right now?

Williams: Right now she's screaming at me, but the poison takes a while to work.

Operator: Is that your girlfriend I hear in the background?

Williams: That's her. She's saying she doesn't need an ambulance, but believe me, she does. She needs to get her stomach pumped, right away.

Operator: Paramedics will be there soon.

It sure seemed like Theo had tried his best to get help for his girlfriend. It was hard to believe he had intended to poison her based on his quick reaction.

The next document was a copy of Theo's phone records, showing that he'd texted or called Courtney three dozen times after she'd left his home that evening. After that was a copy of Courtney's medical records from her visit to the hospital later that night, but the document was so redacted it was effectively useless. There was also a copy of a report from the police department's drug enforcement team, estimating the value and potency of the marijuana plants Theo had been growing.

That was it. Nothing about the deal he'd accepted or what the specifics of his sentence were. Still, what she'd read gave Julia a very different way to think about Theo. He seemed like a smart kid. An awkward kid, and one with some strange interests and proclivities. But it did seem like, if these records were to be believed, he probably hadn't intentionally poisoned his girlfriend.

Did that mean he hadn't planted the plants in Forsyth Park though? Julia couldn't be sure. He had knowledge of the plants, and based on what she'd read, she could imagine him thinking it was some kind of strange social experiment. She didn't think he'd poisoned his girlfriend, but she couldn't cross him off the list for Forsyth Park yet.

She realized she would need to talk to Theo again, this time without Professor Elmore there. She went to the website for Savannah State. It wasn't hard to decipher the email format: firstname.lastname@savannahstate.edu. She sent emails to both Theo Williams and Theodore Williams, just in case, asking if they could meet, and then she closed the email from Barbara and sat back.

She was pretty sure Calvin Corliss was their man, but she still wanted to talk with Theo. She would have to hope he would write her back. For now, it was time to get going if she wanted to catch Calvin Corliss.

***

Just past five, Julia packed up her things and said goodbye to Carmen, who was shutting down her computer, and then she got into her car and programmed the GPS to 42 Briarpatch Lane in Pooler. Traffic moved slowly at this time, so she listened to classical music as she made her way through the streets of the suburb. The houses in Pooler were not huge, but most were on the newer side, and the subdivision where Calvin Corliss lived was well kept, with wide sidewalks and neatly mown lawns. All those HOA rules paid off, she supposed. She found the house easily enough, a two-story wood-frame with a large front window and a wide garage door. There were no cars in the driveway, and no lights on inside that she could see, but she parked in front and went up the cement path to the front door. She rang the doorbell, but there was no answer. He was probably still at work. Well, it had been worth a try.

She went back to her car and tried to figure out her next steps. How could she find out more about Calvin? How could she prove that he was the one behind the plants in Forsyth Park?

While Julia sat thinking, a car turned onto the street, slowed, and turned in to the driveway. She watched as Calvin stepped out of the car and walked up the pathway and into the house.

Well, now. That was good timing. Julia sat in her car a moment, giving him time to get settled and also allowing herself time to work out how she would approach him. Then she climbed out of the car and walked up the path to the front door. She pressed the doorbell and heard it ring inside, and a moment later Calvin Corliss stood in the open doorway.

"Yeah?"

"Hello. My name is Julia Foley, and I'm interested in learning about some plants."

"Okay…"

It had sounded better in her head.

"Am I right in thinking that you work for the parks department?"

"Who did you say you are again?"

"Julia Foley."

He looked around, as if checking to make sure none of the neighbors was watching. "Why don't you come in."

"Thank you." Julia stepped inside. "This is lovely." The house had an airy two-level entryway, with a room that looked like an office off to the left. To the right was an open living room, with an oversized leather couch and recliners. The walls were beige, and the carpet was beige, and the leather couch was tan. A television played the news quietly in the corner of the room.

"Thanks." He was a big guy, but he seemed to not know what to do with his arms.

A fireplace was set against the interior wall, and photos and various antiques were scattered along the top.

"What did you say you needed?"

Julia tried again. "I'm looking for some advice on plants, specifically ones called datura stramonium and atropa belladonna."

He stared at her blankly.

"Since you work for the parks department, I was hoping you might be able to help me learn more about those particular plants." Julia saw an antique pistol displayed on the mantel, and next to it was a sword in a scabbard. It was old, though she couldn't say how old.

"I don't really work with the plants. I just mow the lawns and bag up garbage."

"But surely you must know something about plants. You don't do any gardening?"

Julia looked at the photos on the mantel. There was a school photo of a gap-toothed girl with strawberry-blond hair, probably around six. And there was a candid shot of a dark-haired boy who was maybe four or five.

"I don't really have much time for gardening. And I've never heard of those plants you mentioned."

Julia decided to stop beating around the bush.

"But I've seen you at Forsyth Park, walking around where those plants are growing, wearing a belt full of gardening supplies."

"I don't go to Forsyth Park." He said it so definitely that, for a moment, she doubted herself. Had they been mistaken? But no, it was Randy Torrez who had first mentioned seeing him there, and he knew Calvin. And that was definitely him in the security camera footage.

"Actually, I have—"

"I think it's time for you to leave." His tone, which had been wary, now turned threatening. Julia understood that he wasn't messing around, and given his appreciation for weapons, she didn't want to overstay her welcome. But she did take one more run at it as she walked toward the door.

"I have video footage. I'm just trying to understand what—"

"Get. Out. Now."

Julia didn't argue this time. She scurried out the door and hopped into her car. She didn't exactly peel out of the parking space, but it was close. Her heartbeat didn't slow down until she was out of the housing development and back on the highway headed home.

That hadn't gone as she'd hoped. But she'd learned that he was hiding something. A person didn't react like that unless they really didn't want to talk about what they knew. Sure, he had denied knowing anything about the plants, but he had also denied ever going to Forsyth Park, and she knew for a fact he did go there, regularly.

Her phone rang and she answered it by pressing the button on her steering wheel.

"How did it go?" Meredith asked. Julia filled her in on the visit. "I'm glad you got out of there when you did," Meredith said.

"I don't think he would have actually hurt me," Julia said. "But he was certainly clear that he wanted me to go."

"I don't know. If we're right, and he's responsible for those plants, he must have a plan to hurt someone with them. You never know what people are capable of."

"I suppose you're right," Julia admitted.

"Do you think we should let the police see the footage?" Meredith asked. "And point them toward Calvin?"

"I was wondering the same thing," Julia said. Judging by the length of time it had taken them to come to search the area for evidence, they didn't seem to be particularly invested in this case, and Julia could see, from their perspective, why some plants in a park rated lower on the priority list than the crime that was a constant throughout the city. Maybe this would be what they needed to take this case seriously.

"I can't go by the station now, because I have company coming for dinner," Julia said. "But we can go tomorrow. I think we know who our mysterious gardener is."

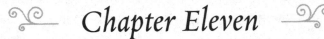

Chapter Eleven

JULIA WAS GETTING THINGS READY for Wyatt and his children, who were due to arrive shortly, when her phone rang. It was a local number but one she didn't recognize.

"Hello?"

"Hi, Ms. Foley? This is Lynley. From the dean's office?"

"Yes, hello, Lynley."

"I heard back from Heather. My old roommate who is in the Eco Club? She didn't have any kind of official list of people in the Eco Club, but she listed the ones she could think of for me."

"That's wonderful." Julia grabbed a pen and notebook from the junk drawer. "Go ahead."

"Okay. Hunter Whitehead. Jenn Nguyen. Felix Levine. Angela Gilkie. Kaitlyn McCrae. Aarti Bagla. Melissa Zacharia. Malika Watson. And Uriah Stine."

Julia asked her to spell the names out to make sure she had them all right, and then asked, "Do you know any of these people?"

"I was in an English class with Uriah. He never read the assignments and seemed hungover most of the time. And Melissa is also a film major, but she's a year behind me, so I don't really know her. And I met Felix once at a party, but I doubt he'd remember me. The others… No, I don't know them at all."

"So you don't know if any of them know about poisonous plants?"

"I'm afraid not. But, you know, it's pretty clear that the video you showed me shows a girl, so you can discount half of these names right off the bat."

"Good point," Julia said. "Thank you. This is very helpful."

"Okay, I have to run, but let me know if you need anything else." Lynley hung up.

Julia wanted to dive into research, but their guests would be here soon and she needed to get things ready. She carried a stack of paper plates and napkins out to the picnic table. Beau had already fired up the grill and set ketchup and mustard out on the table in the backyard. He had a plate of hamburger patties ready to cook and was wearing the Kiss the Cook apron he always wore when he manned the grill.

"Thank you for getting things started," Julia said as she carried a tray of glasses out to the back deck.

"You're welcome. I always appreciate the opportunity to play with fire," Beau said. "But you haven't followed instructions." He pointed to his apron.

Julia laughed and set the glasses down then leaned in and planted a kiss on his cheek. She returned to the kitchen and was just about to carry a pitcher of lemonade outside when the doorbell rang again and again and again, and then Kennedy and Madison flew inside.

"Hi, Nana!" seven-year-old Kennedy said. "Look at my tooth. It's wiggly." She pushed on the front tooth with her tongue.

"My goodness. That's almost ready to come out, isn't it?" Julia asked.

"And Nana, see my bruise? I fell off my bike." Six-year-old Madison pointed to a purple spot on her leg.

"You must have taken quite a tumble," Julia said.

"Yeah, but I can ride with no training wheels, just like Kennedy." Madison's hands were on her hips, her chest stuck out proud.

Wyatt came in, carrying a bowl of fruit, and Anna Beth held a plate covered with foil. She leaned in and gave Julia a kiss on the cheek. "It's good to see you," Julia said. "You can take that right on out to the back." Wyatt set the fruit salad down and gave her a hug.

She turned to the kids. "If you go out to the backyard, you'll find something for each of you." They ran out the back door, Kennedy just a bit ahead of Madison, and squealed when they saw the electric bubble wands she'd put on the picnic table for them.

Julia followed the girls out and showed them how to turn the wands on, and soon bubbles and shrieks of laughter filled the backyard. Julia chatted with Anna Beth about the day camps the kids were attending later that summer, Beau started cooking the burgers, and they were almost ready to eat when Cassie appeared in the doorway, carrying a bowl.

"Hi there," she said and leaned in to give Julia a kiss on the cheek. "I hope it's okay that I let myself in. No one answered the door."

"That's quite all right." It hadn't really occurred to Julia to have someone inside to listen for the door. Family always just came on in.

Julia gestured for her to come out, and Cassie stepped into the backyard. Julia walked over and took the bowl from her hands. "Is this macaroni salad? That was thoughtful."

"Grandma!" Madison set down her bubble wand and ran over to hug Cassie just like she'd run to Julia. Julia tried not to let it bother her. Cassie *was* their grandmother after all. Even though Julia thought of them as her grandchildren and had been the closest thing to a grandmother in their lives, Cassie was, technically, their grandmother.

Anna Beth gestured for Cassie and Julia to come toward her, and she continued the conversation about the kids' summer activities, and then turned to Julia.

"I heard you've signed up to run the 5K. I was so excited to see that."

"Yes, well." Julia let out an awkward laugh. "We'll see if I survive it."

"Of course you'll survive it. You'll do great." Cassie swatted her concern away. "How's your training going?"

"Oh, you know. It's not my favorite thing," Julia said. "But I'm doing it."

"How many miles are you up to?" Anna Beth asked.

Julia didn't really want to talk about this, but they were both waiting for her to share, so she said, "Almost two miles this morning. Two slow miles, that is."

"That's okay," Anna Beth said. "It's so great that you're getting out there and doing it."

"I haven't been able to run at all this week, I've been so busy," Cassie said. "I sure hope I can get some runs in before the race, or who knows what will happen."

Julia felt her shoulders tense, and she made herself take a long, slow breath before she answered. "You're doing it, though, right? You're not going to flake out on me, are you?"

Cassie's eyes widened. Anna Beth pressed her lips together, and that was how Julia realized the words had come out more harshly than she'd intended.

"No. I'm not going to flake out on you," Cassie said. "I'm going to be there, just like I said I would."

"Okay," Julia said. There were so many things running through her head, but she didn't trust herself to say any of them out loud. Anna Beth's eyes were darting from one to the other, panic in her face.

"You don't believe me." Cassie sounded—well, she looked crushed. "You really think I'm not going to come through."

"You have to admit, it wouldn't be the first time," Julia said.

"Excuse me," Anna Beth said quietly and then stepped away, leaving just the two sisters face-to-face.

"That's fair," Cassie said calmly, though it was clear the words stung. "I can see why you'd say that. I haven't always been there for you, and for Mom and Dad and Wyatt. But Julia, I'm not that person anymore. Or at least, I'm trying not to be." She took in a breath and let it out before she continued. "I know there's a lot of water under the bridge, and I'm not saying it's not important. I'm just saying, I'm here now, and I'm determined that I'm not going to let you down again."

Julia wanted to believe her. She really did. But experience had taught her to be wary.

"Okay. So you promise you'll be at the 5K?"

"Yes," Cassie said. "I promise I'll be at the 5K. But I meant more than that."

Julia felt the ache of tears beginning to build in the back of her throat, and she pressed her lips together.

"I'm here to stay, Julia. I'm not leaving again. I know you think I'm flaky, and that I can't be trusted, but what I'm trying to get you to see is that that's not me anymore. I mean, I get why you think that about me. I'm self-aware enough to understand that it's not coming from nowhere. But I've been doing a lot of work on myself, and I hope you can believe me when I say I've changed. I'm not going to abandon you all again. I'm not going to skip out on the race, and I'm not going away. I'm here to stay."

Julia wanted to believe it. She wanted with every bit of herself to be able to trust Cassie. She could see that Wyatt and the kids had let her in, to some degree anyway. But she wasn't sure she was able to just yet. She wasn't sure she was ready to risk having her heart broken again. She nodded, but she didn't know what to say.

She was glad when, just then, Beau called out, "The burgers are ready! Who's hungry?"

The kids ran toward the table, screeching. Wyatt and Anna Beth glanced over at Julia and Cassie, as if unsure whether to approach.

"I know I have to earn your trust back," Cassie said. "But I'm committed to doing whatever it takes."

Julia took a deep breath and said, "Okay, then. If you're willing to try, so am I."

"Thank you, Julia." Cassie's shoulders relaxed. "And when I said this 5K was something we could do together, I meant it. Could we do a training run together? Maybe Saturday morning?"

After all that, Julia didn't know how she could refuse.

"Okay," she said. "Saturday morning it is."

***

After their guests had gone, Julia decided to do some research on the names Lynley had given her. She started by eliminating the names that were clearly boys from the list and focused on the names that remained: Jenn Nguyen, Angela Gilkie, Kaitlyn McCrae, Aarti Bagla, Melissa Zacharia, and Malika Watson.

Julia wasn't sure about the name Aarti, so she started there. She googled the name and found an Instagram account for a beautiful young woman from California, whom Julia guessed was of Indian and Pakistani descent. Aarti was a fashion major at SCAD, and her Instagram was full of gorgeous shots of Aarti wearing outfits that Julia didn't understand. Why would you wear jeans with a dress? What was the point of a thick wool sweater over cut-off shorts? But judging by the comments on the photos, others found her outfits "inventive" and "daring" and "gorgeous!" But Julia didn't find anything at all to link her to plants of any kind. Julia didn't know what she'd been hoping for—a photo of the woman posing with a pot of monkshoods, maybe—but there was nothing to make Julia either suspect her or clear her.

She typed in the name JENN NGUYEN, but that turned out to be a very common name, and she wasn't sure how to figure out which was the right profile. But Julia was pretty sure the name Nguyen was Vietnamese, and the girl they'd seen in the video had light brown hair, so she thought it was unlikely to be her. Still, you couldn't make assumptions, so she kept digging for a while longer before she gave up and moved on the next name, Angela Gilkie.

She found an Instagram profile for an Angela Gilkie who was an accountant in Minneapolis, and another for a young woman from Queens, New York. The second woman seemed younger, based on her profile picture. She had dirty blond hair and round cheeks, with beautiful green eyes. Julia studied the photo. She could be the girl in the video, she thought. She was the right build, though it was still really hard to say. She scrolled through the photos and found a selfie of Angela in front of the Tybee Island Lighthouse from last fall. Bingo. She was in Savannah. This had to be the right Angela Gilkie, Julia thought. But she couldn't find anything about her online that would tie her to the plants in the garden.

Kaitlyn McCrae had almost no digital footprint, at least not that Julia could see, but she found a few TikTok videos of Malika Watson dancing. Melissa Zakaria liked to pose for pictures with a pug and also liked to photograph everything she ate.

Julia was grasping at straws, she realized. She was pinning all of her hopes for finding the person who had planted those flowers on that one woman in the video footage. There had to be other possibilities. What was she missing?

She was getting bleary-eyed and worked up, so she decided to call it a night. But first, she sent the list of names and the research she'd done so far to Meredith. Maybe she would see something Julia had missed.

Chapter Twelve

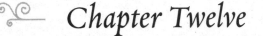

Eugenia,

Thank you for your kind note. It has been difficult since Edward passed. For so many years whenever he frustrated me, I'd wonder what it would be like to be free of him, but the truth is, it's miserable. I had gotten used to him, I suppose, despite his peculiarities. It's hard to see his side of the table empty.

It has been some comfort to have Lily and Charles here. Lily and I have had our disagreements, you know that, but she and Edward always had a special relationship, and she is mourning him deeply. It has been such a comfort to have her here through all of this, and of course I love having little Ellen and Merritt here as well. They bring joy in a dark time.

In regard to your question, yes, I had heard about how Marie Brownlee was able to save Adeline from the river. Myrtle told me all about it and praised the training Marie had received in Daisy's club for knowing what to do. Though I did not appreciate her smug tone, I suppose I can admit that there has been some good to come out of that club. Let's hope there isn't need for that particular skill to be exercised again anytime soon.

Yours,

Hattie

Julia woke up Friday morning to find two text messages from Meredith on her screen: ANGELA GILKIE. And the second: WATCH THIS, followed by a link. Meredith had sent the texts just after midnight. What had she been doing up at that time? Julia clicked on the link, and a browser window opened to YouTube. She clicked to start the video, and saw that it featured Angela, whom she recognized from her own research. She was in what looked like a bedroom and was seated at a table covered with small diffusers and a bunch of oranges. What in the world?

"Hi there, and welcome back. I want to talk to you today about citrus—"

Beau rolled over, and Julia silenced the video and crept out of the bedroom. She put the coffeepot on and, as the machine hissed and sputtered, sat down at the table. Bunny meowed and rubbed against Julia's leg. Julia obediently picked up the cat and stroked her head until Bunny purred. Then Julia started the video over and watched it. How had she missed this in her own research on Angela?

"Hi there, and welcome back. I want to talk to you today about citrus notes," Angela said. "Citrus notes are, as you would expert, fresh, fruity, and light, and are generally top notes in a fragrance. In the perfume world, we call these the hesperdic fruits, after the Hesperides, which are nymphs in Greek mythology. Citruses provide a refreshing or effervescent quality to fragrances, and they feel sunny and optimistic and give a sense of cleanness and energy. In this video, I'll tell you about some of my favorites."

Julia tried to make sense of this. Angela was doing a video about...fragrances?

"The most obvious citrus is orange," Angela said, reaching for an orange on the table. "It's sweet, with a small facet of astringency." She stopped and picked up one of the small diffusers in front of her and sprayed a fine mist into the air. "It's lovely, but it's a bit...well, obvious. There are so many other more interesting citruses out there. Take yuzu, for instance. Yuzu is a smaller, yellow citrus fruit originally from China, and it has a sweet yet very bitter fragrance. It adds depth and gives your scent just a little bit of edge. You find yuzu showing up in many foods and drinks these days, but the fruit itself is not easy to find. Still, the scent is fresh, but with an attitude."

Julia supposed she'd never really considered the different scents in perfumes before. She'd been wearing *L'Air du Temp* since her grandmother had given her a bottle on her sixteenth birthday and told her a woman needed a signature scent. Every year for Christmas Beau bought her a new bottle, and she hadn't really thought about it beyond that.

"Now, bergamot is one of my favorite scents in any profile. Many people are surprised to learn bergamot is actually a citrus fruit, because they associate it with tea. It's what gives Earl Grey tea that earthy, sweet richness. But bergamot actually comes from a small green fruit that grows in Italy and on the southern coast of France. I don't have any here, because it's hard to find in Georgia, but it's a complex spice, citrusy and earthy, all at once."

Julia watched as Angela went on to talk about the fragrance notes of grapefruit and lemongrass, and then she directed her viewers to leave their thoughts in the comments. The video ended, and Julia set the phone down and sat back. That was interesting. She had to admit she'd learned things she hadn't known, and listening to Angela talk about fragrance notes was actually kind of soothing. But what did it have to do with anything?

Julia set Bunny down on the floor before she got up and poured herself a cup of coffee. She also tossed some food into Bunny's dish, and when the cat dove for the food, Julia sat back down and looked at her screen again. She looked at the YouTube page the video was embedded in and saw that this was Angela's YouTube channel. Or, more precisely, a channel called Scents and Scentsability. A Jane Austen fan, Julia surmised. She had dozens of videos and more than two hundred subscribers, which surprised Julia. There was a short description of the channel at the top. *Fragrance fiend. Herbalist and nature lover. I share about my passion for how natural ingredients make the world a more lovely place.*

Huh. Julia wasn't really sure what to make of that. She checked the time. It was probably still too early to call Meredith, so she selected another video from the list and watched as Angela talked about the fragrance notes of resins, like myrrh and frankincense, as well as several Julia had never heard of, including dragon blood resin. They all, Angela promised, added depth and woodiness and "a lingering trail" to a fragrance.

The next video was about balsams, followed by musks and then berries. Julia had had no idea there were so many different kinds of scents that could be incorporated into a fragrance or perfume. And she hadn't even started on the florals yet. Still, she wasn't quite sure what had gotten Meredith so excited. Julia could see that Angela knew a lot about plants, and she was in the Eco Club, which made her a person of interest to be sure, but what had made Meredith send her this link so late last night?

It was just past eight now. Surely Meredith would be up. Julia poured herself another cup of coffee and called Meredith. It rang twice and went to voice mail.

HANG ON, Meredith texted immediately.

Julia watched another video while she waited, and then jumped when her phone rang.

"Did you see it?" Meredith asked by way of greeting.

"I saw a lot of videos about perfume. But I'm not sure exactly what I was supposed to see."

"What do you mean? You saw the video I sent, right?"

"Yes. It was a video about citrus notes by Angela, who is one of our prime suspects."

"Citrus? It was about flowers."

"No, the link you sent went to a video about oranges and things."

"Argh. That's the wrong one. I saw that one, but I meant to send you the one about flowers. Hang on. I'll send it again."

"How did you even find these?" Julia asked. "I don't see her name listed anywhere on the page, so it didn't come up while I was searching."

"I spent way too much time going way too deep into the void of the internet after Chase and the kids went to bed," Meredith said. "I found out all kinds of things. First off, did you know that you can major in Beauty and Fragrance at SCAD?"

"Like, makeup and perfume?"

"Apparently. I think it's more about the business aspects of the beauty and fragrance industries, but yes. Angela mentions in one of her early videos that she's in that program. Apparently she started doing these videos for a class assignment."

"But she kept doing them."

"Maybe there's money to be made in this kind of thing. You hear enough about online influencers these days. I don't know. Maybe she just likes talking about something she loves. Anyway, in another one of her videos she also mentions the power of herbs and supplements. Plants."

"Okay."

"She's here in Savannah for the summer. The most recent video she posted was from last week, and she was in the same room she was in in the first video, from December. It's got to be her dorm room, or off-campus housing, or wherever she lives during the school year. And she's got to be here in town still if she's filming from the same location."

Now that Meredith mentioned it, the room Angela filmed in did look like a dorm room. Julia hadn't paid a lot of attention to the background before, but it was a small narrow room with a bed and not much else.

"She knows a lot about flowers," Meredith said.

"That's true." Everything Meredith said was true, but it all seemed pretty circumstantial to Julia. Yes, Angela was certainly a possibility. She looked enough like the girl in the security camera footage that it could be her. She was also in the Eco Club, so that was another link. But... Julia felt that Calvin Corliss was the stronger suspect. And there was still Theo Williams.

"Okay, I just sent you the video I intended to send you last night. Take a look. I have to go get breakfast for the kids, but I'll be in later. Chase is going to take the kids to the pool this morning."

"That sounds great. I'll watch this video, and then I'll get breakfast and head into the office."

"Talk to you later."

A moment later, another text from Meredith came through, with a different link, and when she clicked on it, she was taken to the Scents and Scentsability YouTube channel again.

"Hi again. Thanks for tuning in once more, and I'm so glad you're here." Angela was in the same bedroom, with the same set of little bottles and diffusers around her, as well as some flowers. "Today, we're going to be talking about white florals, which is a sub-category of florals. White florals are an important group of scent notes, and they are some of the most lush, opulent, and intoxicating scents you'll find. They are intensely feminine. I wanted to talk to you about some of my favorites today."

In the video, Angela went on to talk about orange blossom, which she described as "a fresh and sweet white floral with animalic undertones." She talked about growing up in Central Florida among the orange groves and the heady smell of orange blossoms in the springtime. Then she picked up one of the diffusers, sprayed it, and sniffed the fine mist that fell around her. "It's so intensely feminine and sweet," she said before putting the diffuser back down.

She then picked up a peach stargazer lily and held it up to the camera. "I just love the scent of lilies. This is obviously not a white lily, but it's what I could find, and the scent is similar—sweet, waxy, spicy. It's intense, and one of the most powerful of the florals."

Then she set the lily down and talked about honeysuckle and jasmine before she picked up—

Oh my.

Julia's heartbeat sped up. She saw why exactly Meredith had sent her the video. And it changed everything.

Chapter Thirteen

JULIA SAT DOWN AT HER desk Friday morning with a plan. They had three good suspects, and she intended to figure out today which of them was the one who had planted the flowers in Forsyth Park. Later today, they would wait for Calvin Corliss, assuming he showed up as he had the past two Friday afternoons. When Meredith got in, they would both try to talk to Theo Williams to find out more about the poisoning incident. And in the meantime, Julia was determined to learn more about Angela Gilkie.

First, she went back to the video Meredith had sent her, the one where Angela was talking about white florals. She fast-forwarded to the part she wanted to see again.

"This is the flower commonly known as datura," Angela explained in the video. She picked up the now-familiar white flower, leaned in, and sniffed it deeply. "It comes in pure white, but it also grows in the most beautiful white and purple mix. It's not too common, because parts of the plant are toxic to dogs and children, but its scent is gorgeous—sweet, almost magical. Datura is actually used to make many medicines today. And, used as a dietary supplement, it's got so many health benefits—it relieves pain and has anti-inflammatory properties, and is great for stomach problems, toothache, headache, and many other kinds of pain relief."

Angela talked about gardenias and honeysuckle, but Julia was barely listening. Angela had a datura flower, right in front of her in the video. And she obviously knew about both its toxicity and its purported health benefits.

Did that mean she was the one who had planted the garden? Not by any means. But did it mean that she had moved higher up on Julia's list? It did indeed.

She pulled up Angela's YouTube page again and found the most recent video. This was a deep dive into the tropical floral notes in fragrance, such as ylang-ylang, coconut, and frangipani. Julia let it run, but she wasn't really listening to what Angela was saying. Instead, she was focused on observing the room behind Angela. On the left part of the screen was what looked like a built-in wardrobe, and there were clothes draped over the edge of the open door. Next to that was a twin bed covered in a blue and white comforter, and beyond that was a large window. A bulletin board hung over the bed, with photos and papers pinned to it. It looked like a generic dorm room to Julia. She pulled up a map of dorms for the college and found many nearly identical buildings clustered over by the highway. They all looked the same to her. So maybe she couldn't figure out where exactly Angela lived. But there had to be more she could learn from looking at this room. She had to find her somehow. Julia knew that people often revealed things about themselves in their personal space. She just needed to look.

Julia focused on the bulletin board over the bed. Was there anything there that could tell her anything more about how she could track down Angela? Maybe, but the photos were too small, and Julia couldn't read the writing on the pieces of paper that were tacked to the bulletin board.

"What are you up to?"

Julia jumped. "Goodness. You shouldn't sneak up on people."

Meredith laughed. "If you didn't hear these floorboards squeak, you must have been concentrating pretty hard."

"I was. I was watching Angela's videos, trying to find out more about her."

"Did you have any luck?"

"None so far," Julia said.

"If there's anything to be found, you'll find it," Meredith said. "Now, how about we start off the day by talking to your poisonous plant expert."

"Theo Williams?"

"That's right."

"You want to go now?"

"No time like the present," Meredith said. "Besides, I don't know how long I have until I'll need to rescue Chase from the clutches of Kinsley and Kaden."

"Okay," Julia said. "So should we just go confront him in the lab?"

"I was going to suggest we try him at home. It would be easier to talk to him there. Don't college kids keep strange schedules? We might get lucky. And if not, we'll go to the lab."

"I suppose." Julia thought for a moment. "But we don't know where he lives."

Meredith shook her head. "Of course we do. Do you think you're the only one who's good at doing research on our suspects?"

"You have his address?"

"Naturally. How about I drive?"

"Deal."

***

Theo Williams lived in a bungalow not far from the Savannah State campus. The paint was peeling, and the chairs on the porch were cheap molded plastic with grime puddled in the seats. A battered window unit air conditioner hummed in the front window, dripping a steady stream of water onto the floorboards of the porch. Overall, the place had the worn look of seeing too many tenants come and go, and Julia guessed that it, like many of the other houses on the block, was mostly rented by students. The mailbox listed five names for what Julia was sure was not more than a three-bedroom home. Meredith rang the doorbell, but no one answered.

"I hear music inside," Meredith said. "And there are two cars in the driveway." She pointed to the cracked patch of cement along the side of the house, where two beat-up sedans sat. "Someone is here." She pressed the doorbell again, and this time the door was opened by a girl in a T-shirt with Greek letters on it.

"Yeah?"

"We're looking for Theo Williams. Is he available?"

"He's in his room." She moved aside and pulled the door open.

"Where is that exactly?" Meredith asked, stepping inside.

"Very end of the hall." The girl turned and left them there, walking through the living room to some hidden room beyond.

Meredith smiled, and Julia shrugged. They might need to update their security around here, but Julia wasn't going to argue about it now. She followed Meredith past a living room with mismatched furniture and an enormous television and down a hall, past two closed doors and a tiny bathroom, to the door at the end of the hallway. Meredith knocked, and then, when there was no answer, knocked again.

"Come in!"

Meredith pushed open the door. Theo started when he saw them.

"Mrs. Foley?" He sat at a beat-up wooden desk with a large computer monitor.

"Hi, Theo. This is my business partner, Meredith Bellefontaine. We're sorry to barge in like this, but we were hoping you could answer a few questions for us."

The bed was covered with a blue comforter which hadn't been pulled up, and there was a pile of clothes on the floor. Posters of basketball stars were hung on the walls.

"Sure." He pulled out his earbuds, one at a time, and slid them into a white case. "Is this about those plants in Forsyth Park?"

"It is," Julia said. She and Meredith stood awkwardly in the doorway.

"I haven't had a chance to ask my friends on the message boards about the plants," he said.

"That's okay," Julia said. "We really wanted to ask you more about the trouble Professor Elmore mentioned when I met you."

"We saw that your girlfriend had been poisoned by some belladonna you were growing in your bedroom," Meredith said.

"Yeah. That was a bad time." Theo shook his head.

"We were hoping you could tell us about it."

His eyes narrowed. "Wait. You don't think I poisoned her on purpose, do you?" And then, after a moment, he added, "You do. You think I planted those poisonous plants in the park because of my record."

"We want to hear what you have to say," Meredith said calmly.

"I had nothing to do with those plants," Theo said. "Why would I put plants in a public park when I have my own laboratory at the university? I don't need to plant stuff in a park, even if I would plant poisonous plants in a public place, which I would not. Do you know how dangerous that is? Why do you think I study physostigmine?"

"You study what?" Meredith asked.

"It's a reversible cholinesterase inhibitor."

"A what?" Why did scientists speak a whole different language?

"It's an antidote for atropine, the chemical found in atropa belladonna."

When neither of them said anything, he simplified it even further. "I'm working on how to treat people who have been poisoned."

"You are?" Julia definitely hadn't gotten that impression in the lab.

"Yes. What did you *think*?" He tilted his head back. "Did you honestly think I was studying how to *poison people*?"

"We weren't sure," Meredith said quickly. "That's what we came to talk to you. To find out the real story."

"Okay." Theo took a deep breath. "So. Yes, my high school girl-friend did ingest some belladonna I was growing, but it wasn't like I boiled a potion or slipped some poison into her coffee. I was growing the plants because even back then, I was fascinated by poisonous plants."

Julia felt her phone buzz in her purse, but she ignored it. "You were growing the plants in your bedroom, is that right?" she asked.

"Yes," Theo said. "Because I didn't have anywhere else to grow them. Which is not the case now."

"How did she come to ingest the poisonous plant?" Julia had already read about it in the police report, but she wanted to hear Theo's answer.

"My girlfriend was hanging out in my room," Theo said. "And she got mad, because she wanted me to go out to a party but I was trying to finish up some work. We got into a fight, and she was kind of cuckoo if you know what I mean, and she grabbed a bunch of the berries from a belladonna plant and ate them. I don't know why she did it. You'd have to ask her. I guess she thought she'd be punishing me. I called 911 and tried to get her help right away, because, hello, I study that plant and know what it can do to you. I didn't poison her. She did that all on her own."

"She survived, I read," Julia said. "But what happened after you called 911?"

"She refused to go to the hospital. I told you, she was cuckoo. She went home, and I kept texting her, calling her, telling her to go get checked out. It wasn't until she started to get really ill that night that her parents took her in."

"We read that the police got involved," Meredith said.

"Yes, Courtney's father called them after she was hospitalized. He wanted someone to blame for his daughter's stupid actions, I guess. And it was no secret he had never liked me, so I guess I was an easy target."

"Why didn't he like you?" Julia asked.

"Take your pick: race, class, social standing. And then there's the fact that she was only with me so she could supply the whole school with pot, so that didn't count in my favor either."

"Whoa." There was a lot to unpack in that outburst. "Hang on. Go back to the race, class, social standing bit."

"I mean, Courtney was this spoiled rich girl, right? Her dad owned a law firm in town, and she was head cheerleader and all that. I'm, well, I come from a different place, let's just say that. The crazy thing is how long it took me to figure out why she was so interested in hanging out with me. I honestly thought for a while she really just liked me for me, you know, like in one of those movies? It feels silly to even say it now, because it's so obvious what was really going on."

"The poisonous plants weren't the only ones you were growing in your room," Meredith said.

Julia put a finer point on it. "She was interested in the marijuana plants you were growing."

"Yep. A buddy of mine knew about the plants, and I should've known it wouldn't take long for news like that to spread all over school. I guess Courtney figured out that if she pretended to like me, she could come to my place and swipe a few buds off the plants when she thought I wasn't looking."

"Did you notice?"

"Of course I did. I take very good care of my plants, and I notice everything about them. But I figured it wasn't a bad trade-off for getting to date the prettiest girl in the school."

"What were you intending to do with the marijuana plants you grew?" Meredith asked.

"It's funny, people asked me that so many times after I was arrested. Because, as you already know, once Courtney's dad called the cops on me for 'poisoning' his daughter, they found the plants I was growing and that's when I got in real trouble. The thing is, I didn't have a plan. I was just interested in the chemical structure of the plants."

"The chemical structure?" Meredith raised an eyebrow.

"Tetrahydrocannabinol is fascinating—"

"That's okay." Julia held up her hand. "We don't need the chemistry of it. What you're saying is that you grew the illegal and very valuable plants because you were interested in the chemical structure?"

"Yeah." And then, "No one believed me then either. I can't give you a better answer than that, I'm afraid, because it's the truth." Theo opened the cap of his earbud holder and then snapped it back into place. "In any case, the judge took pity on me. I was facing serious jail time, but I pled guilty, and the judge saw that education, not incarceration, would be the most helpful for me, so he sentenced me to college instead of prison."

"And you went," Meredith said.

"I excelled, and I put the past behind me and promised to do my part to make the world safer. After seeing what happened to Courtney after she ate those berries, I decided to work on better treatments. So here I am."

Julia glanced at Meredith and could see that she was feeling the same way she was: convinced he was telling the truth.

"Okay," Julia said.

"Thank you for your time," Meredith said.

"Not a problem," Theo said. He stood and escorted them to the front door.

Once they were back inside Meredith's car, Meredith pulled on her seat belt and leaned her head against the headrest. "So what now?"

Julia took her phone out of her purse to pull up directions and saw that a voice mail had come in while they'd been talking with Theo.

"Maggie Lu wants us to come by the library."

"In that case, we'd better go," Meredith said.

Chapter Fourteen

Eugenia,

I was so sorry to hear about your husband's nephew. The world has gone mad, and it's such a shame that so many good men are being sent halfway around the world to fight such a silly war. I am so sorry for your loss. Let's all pray that this war ends soon and that things can go back to the way they were before quickly.

Things have been much the same here. Butter and sugar are impossible to come by, and there are no parties these days. It's just dreadful. At least we haven't had any shortages of fresh fruits and vegetables. Did you hear what Daisy's girls have been up to? They have planted vegetable gardens—they are calling them Victory Gardens—all over empty lots throughout Savannah. They have been giving the produce away to anyone who needs it. Can you believe it? I've always said those clubs of hers were doing good in the world, and now everyone in town can see it too.

Please send news from Charleston. We're dying for something interesting to happen. Please forgive that thoughtless phrase, I hadn't realized what I was writing, you know how I am sometimes. Sending my love to your family in this dark time.

Hattie

Maggie Lu was reshelving books in the fiction section when Julia and Merdith walked into the library.

"Hello there," she said, sliding a book into place. Julia could see that it was a mystery by an author she liked. "You made it."

Maggie Lu straightened up, holding onto the nearby cart as she stood tall.

"We came as soon as we got your message," Meredith said.

Maggie Lu chuckled. "I knew you would. You two are like a dog with a bone when you're working on a mystery. Come with me. I'll show you what I found."

Maggie Lu led them into a room at the back of the first floor marked Special Collections. She indicated that they should sit at the table in the middle of the room. Then Maggie Lu walked to a low bookshelf and took a large manila envelope from it and set it on the table. She went back and picked up a book, which Julia recognized as the restricted book they'd seen before. Then she sat down, set the book down, and picked up the envelope. She opened up the clasp and pulled out what looked like several very old letters encased in plastic.

"After you all left the other day, I was thinking about what you were talking about, with those poisonous plants and all, and I remembered something I'd read a long time ago. So I pulled it out and wanted to show it to you."

"Maggie Lu, what are those?" Julia asked.

"Granny Luv worked in the home of the Wilson family for a while when I was young."

Julia nodded. Granny Luv was Maggie Lu's grandmother, who had raised her.

"Granny Luv was cleaning out a storage room when she came across a collection of letters kept by Eugenia Wilson, who was the grandmother of the man that owned the house by then. She showed the letter to Charise Wilson, the lady of the house, but Charise didn't want to bother with them, so she told Granny Luv to get rid of them. Well, Granny Luv was smart enough to take them home and hold on to them, just in case."

"Just in case of what?" Meredith asked.

Maggie Lu waited a moment, and then said. "Just in case. You never know what people will reveal in their personal correspondence. It doesn't hurt to have… Well, it doesn't hurt to have records on hand."

When Maggie Lu pressed her lips together and didn't say more, Julia understood that was all they were going to get on the subject. "I found them many years later, and I recognized the significance of the letters, which is why they're in this special collection now. But what I wanted to show you was this."

She pulled the top letter off the stack and held it up. "Eugenia Wilson was a scion in Savannah, from a very wealthy family, and she considered herself something of an arbiter of taste. Her husband, Oscar, was in shipping, and for a while the family moved to Charleston for his work, but they eventually moved back to Savannah. These are letters Eugenia received from her friend Hattie Sinclair in the period when the Wilsons were in Charleston."

Julia could see that Meredith was itching to get her hands on those letters. Meredith had been the president of the Savannah Historical Society for many years and loved old letters from historical time periods in Savannah.

"This is from a letter Hattie sent to Eugenia in 1916." Maggie Lu adjusted her glasses and began to read. "'Has the miracle drug belladonna made it to Charleston yet? Many of us here in town have been using the drops, and with great results. It really does improve one's appearance. I highly recommend you try it.'"

"Some friend," Meredith said, chuckling.

"Yes, Hattie Sinclair does not come across as the most sensitive person in these letters," Maggie Lu said. "But what interested me was that she was apparently using belladonna for beauty. Wasn't that one of the plants you were researching?"

"That's right," Julia said.

"Well, in this book I showed you a few days ago"—she put her hand on the book—"it says that the name belladonna is actually Italian for 'beautiful lady.' It was so named because drops made from the plant were used to dilate women's pupils, which was thought to make them more attractive."

Meredith nodded. "When I was doing research online, I read that it blocks receptors in the eye that constrict the size of the pupil. It fell out of fashion when they realized that prolonged use caused visual distortion and even blindness."

Maggie Lu shuffled through the papers. "Eugenia Wilson was nearly blind by the time she died, according to Granny Luv. She certainly stopped writing letters well before she actually passed, and that could be a reason why."

Julia was interested to learn all of this, but she couldn't understand what Maggie Lu's point in showing them all of this had been. "This is really interesting," she said. "But we already knew that some of the plants were used for medicinal reasons."

"You knew that." Maggie Lu nodded. "But did you *really* know that?"

Julia didn't know what to say. What did she mean?

"Let me say that another way," Maggie Lu said. "You know that those plants you found in the park can be used for medicinal reasons, not just for poison. But are you considering that in your investigation?"

"You mean, maybe whoever planted those plants didn't want them for their poisonous qualities," Meredith said slowly. "You're suggesting that perhaps someone is using the plants for some other reason."

Julia began to understand what Maggie Lu was saying. Now that she had pointed it out, it seemed so obvious. Meredith asked for permission to see the letter, and Maggie Lu handed it to her.

"You've been looking at those plants as dangerous," Maggie Lu said. "All I'm suggesting is that sometimes, things aren't all bad or all good. Sometimes—most of the time, I would say—it's a little bit of both all mixed up together."

"We need to broaden our thinking about the potential reason these plants were put in the park," Julia said slowly.

"It's just a suggestion," Maggie Lu said. "I don't know. It just seems that maybe you're not finding what you're looking for because you're not seeing the whole picture. You've got your own blind spots, so to speak."

"Maggie Lu, you are a genius." Julia couldn't believe they hadn't seen it before. They had been so focused on the idea of poison that they hadn't stopped to consider that there might be another reason the plants were there.

"Are there more of these letters?" Meredith asked, looking up.

"You saw it too, didn't you?" Maggie Lu grinned at her.

"Saw what?" What was Julia missing?

"Listen to this. This is from Hattie, May 1916: 'Vera's grand-daughter Polly came with her when they came by last week. We took a stroll around the garden, and Polly was able to identify all the flowers and the varieties of ferns. I was quite impressed. Polly said she learned it all from her involvement with Daisy's club. Daisy calls the girls "Scouts" now, which makes it all seem rather wild, if you ask me. But I will admit that it does seem as though they are learn-ing more than I first gave them credit for.'"

Meredith set the letter down. "Is this *the* Daisy?"

Maggie Lu nodded. "It is indeed. All the letters in this batch make reference to Daisy and the club for girls she was starting."

"Wait." Julia understood suddenly. "Daisy, as in Juliette Gordon Low?"

Julia had grown up in Savannah, hometown of the founder of the Girl Scouts. Juliette Gordon Low's nickname had been Daisy and the youngest group of Girl Scouts was named after her.

"That's the one." Maggie Lu was smiling. "I pulled these letters out and kept them because they are contemporaneous accounts of the first Girl Scout troop."

Julia pulled the next letter in the stack toward herself and read through it. "Wow. This one is complaining about how the girls were learning to sleep outside 'like savages.'"

"Quite possibly the very first Girl Scout campout," Meredith said quietly.

"Hattie had some strong opinions about the Girl Scouts at first, but she came around," Maggie Lu said.

Julia had briefly been a Girl Scout when she was younger, and like most people in Savannah, she was familiar with the basics of the story. Young Juliette—who sometimes went by her nickname Daisy—traveled to England, where she encountered the British Girl Guides, and decided to establish a similar organization in America. She started with a small group of girls in Savannah. Now there were millions of Girl Scouts learning practical skills and serving their communities around the world. Juliette Gordon Low's home was a major tourist attraction in town, visited by thousands of girls each year with merit badges pinned all over their little vests.

"I'm so glad you saved these," Julia said. "What an amazing treasure."

"I think they're pretty neat as well," Maggie Lu said. "And like I said, at first Hattie thought the Girl Scouts were terrible, but she slowly came around to see that like most things, it wasn't all bad. If you stop focusing on the negative, you just might see some positive elements as well."

"That's very wise advice," Meredith said.

Julia nodded. "I couldn't agree more."

"And you've made one thing very clear," Meredith added. "We have a lot more work to do."

Chapter Fifteen

MEREDITH AND JULIA WENT BACK to the office. They had a bit of time before they had to go to the park to wait for Calvin. Julia answered a few emails before she took out her phone and studied the pictures she'd taken of the flowers back when she'd discovered the hidden garden on Monday. She hadn't seen it before, because she hadn't been looking, but Maggie Lu's advice caused her to see it clearly now. Julia typed out a text, and then she reread it several times before she hesitantly sent it off. Theo Williams had said they could ask him if they had any questions, and, well, she did. She hoped he'd meant it.

A text from Theo appeared on her screen. HAPPY TO HELP. WHAT DO YOU NEED?

She typed back: I'M ATTACHING A PICTURE OF THE GARDEN AS I FOUND IT ON MONDAY. WHEN I SAW YOU ON TUESDAY, YOU IDENTIFIED ANGEL'S-TRUMPET FOXGLOVE, AND BELLADONNA. ANY OTHER PLANTS IN HERE THAT YOU RECOGNIZE? And then she attached the first photo she'd taken on her walk through the park.

Almost immediately, three dots appeared under her message, indicating that Theo was typing a response.

HARD TO TELL FOR SURE, BUT THE ONE IN FRONT OF THE ANGEL'S-TRUMPET LOOKS LIKE ECHINACEA. MIGHT BE GINKGO BILOBA ON THE FAR RIGHT.

Julia had heard of those before. They were both sold as health supplements in drugstores.

THEY AREN'T POISONOUS, ARE THEY? she wrote back.

Theo's response came quickly. IN LARGE ENOUGH DOSES ANYTHING IS POISONOUS. GINKGO SEEDS ARE TOXIC IF INGESTED, BUT GENERALLY NO. THOSE PLANTS ARE NORMALLY GROWN FOR THEIR HEALTH BENEFITS.

Julia thanked Theo and then sat back to think. Maggie Lu was right. Julia had been so focused on the plants that were known to be poisonous that she hadn't considered other plants in the garden, the ones known to have health properties. And didn't even the poisonous plants have health benefits too? That was what that book in the library was about, after all. She'd been so focused on the dangerous properties of the plants that she hadn't considered that perhaps someone was interested in using them for good. It was like Maggie Lu said, she realized. Not everything was all good or all bad; most things had both good qualities and bad qualities mixed together.

Julia closed her eyes. Had the secret garden in the park been planted by someone hoping to harvest the plants for their health benefits? What would have seemed completely ridiculous a few hours ago now seemed entirely plausible. She had been thinking about this whole thing wrong.

"Are you ready?" Meredith had popped her head into Julia's office.

"Ready." She hadn't realized it was already time to head to the park. Julia stood and grabbed her purse and hat before coming around her desk and following Meredith down the hall. They said goodbye to Carmen and stepped outside.

"I was thinking it would make sense to wait on those benches on the corner of Whitaker and Gaston," Julia said, placing the sun hat on her head. "That way we should be able to see him when he comes down Whitaker, but we won't be just standing around on a street corner. We can act like we're just two ladies having a rest on an afternoon stroll."

"That sounds like a good plan to me." Meredith also donned her hat, and they each slipped on sunglasses. They'd agreed that trying to avoid being recognized was a good idea after the way Calvin had reacted to Julia's questions the day before.

The park was busy, with dogs barking and the happy shouts of children as they ran around the playground. Julia and Merdith found an empty bench on the street corner. They were squarely in the shot of the security camera at the house with the big porch, Julia knew, and she had to restrain herself from waving.

While they waited, Meredith told Julia that Quin was taking her and Chase and the kids out for dinner. Julia was glad to see Quin spending more time with Meredith's family, and she wondered, not for the first time, whether their dating relationship would become something more.

"There he is." Meredith nodded at the burly man wearing the same parks department polo as he had in the video footage. He was still a hundred feet away, but it was clearly him.

"Sunglasses and hat, check. And the tool belt as well," Julia said. "It's so brazen, isn't it? He flat-out denied ever coming to Forsyth

Park, and yet here he is, right on schedule." She kept her voice low, even though he was too far away to hear them.

"Let's watch him and see where he goes first and follow him from a distance," Meredith suggested. "That way we can catch him in the garden."

"Good idea," Julia said. "And I'll shoot the whole thing so we have proof."

She pulled her phone out and opened the camera app. She held the camera low, where she hoped it was mostly out of sight. When Calvin got about twenty feet away, she hit the button to start recording. She watched as he walked right past them, not even seeing them—a blessing for which Julia was grateful. When he got about fifteen feet ahead of them, they stood up and began to walk along behind him. He turned into the park midway along the west side, just as they had predicted he would. Julia tried to keep the camera as steady as possible and keep him in the frame as they trailed along behind him.

But when he got to the path that Julia had first taken to find the garden, he didn't turn down it like she thought he would. Instead, he kept walking straight.

"Where's he going?" Meredith whispered. Julia shook her head. Was he going somewhere else before he went to the secret garden? A rollerblader flew down the path, briefly coming between them and Calvin, but Calvin didn't seem to notice. He kept walking and turned onto the main central path that led to the fountain. They followed behind, and then he turned off the main path and followed one that had only one destination.

"He's going to the playground?" Julia asked.

"What in the world?"

Ahead of them, a waist-high gate surrounded a playground with colorful climbing equipment and slides and swings. Julia had brought Madison and Kennedy here several times, and she'd always considered it a safe and well-maintained place for kids to play. But what was Calvin doing here? she wondered. They watched him open the latch on the gate, walk inside, and find a seat on a bench along the outside edge of the playground. They both slowed their steps and waited a moment before following him inside the playground. Meredith and Julia walked directly past Calvin, but he didn't seem to notice, and they found a seat on a bench about twenty feet away from him.

"What is he doing here?" Meredith asked quietly.

"I have no idea." But Julia got a sick feeling in her gut. There were not many reasons a man hid his identity and came alone to a playground.

"You don't think he—"

"I don't know. But why else would he be so careful to hide his identity?" Now that Julia thought about it, several other pieces of the puzzle fell into place. "And it would explain why he got so upset when I asked him about coming to Forsyth Park. He wouldn't want to admit he'd been here if…he had bad motives."

"Is that camera still rolling?" Meredith asked.

"Sure is."

"Good. Let's watch and see what he does."

They sat still a while longer, watching Calvin stare straight ahead, looking at the kids on the playground. What was he looking at so intently? Julia turned her gaze from Calvin to the kids running and swinging and sliding, and then she noticed something.

"Do you see that little boy over there?" Julia pointed to a dark-haired child.

"The one pushing the other kids out of the way on the slide?"

"That's him."

"Okay. So who is he?"

Julia didn't answer, scanning the playground for what she thought she'd see, and—

There it was. And with that piece of evidence, everything she thought she knew about why Calvin was in the park suddenly dissolved.

"Actually, I think I was wrong. I don't think Calvin is guilty after all."

Chapter Sixteen

MEREDITH TURNED HER HEAD. "WHAT do you mean?"

"Those are his kids."

"Who? That boy?"

"That boy and that little girl over there in the pink dress." Julia pointed to the little girl, who was pumping her legs on the swing, her strawberry-blond hair flying out behind her. "I saw their photos on the mantel in his house."

"So you're saying he comes here to stare at his kids?" Meredith looked skeptical.

"Doesn't that look like what he's doing?" Julia tried to think. What had Carmen told her about Calvin? "He was recently involved in a custody battle over the kids. His ex-wife filed a restraining order."

"What's with the gardening tool belt then?"

"Maybe it's part of the disguise." Julia shrugged. "Trying to blend in as a gardener."

"A gardener who sits at the playground and watches kids play?"

"I don't know," Julia said. "That's just my best guess."

"So if there was a restraining order, his ex must have had good reason to be afraid for their safety?"

"I suppose. Maybe. It's hard to say for sure without looking into the case. Sometimes in contentious divorces people take them out for spite."

"Imagine doing that to someone you once promised to love forever."

"Families are complicated," Julia said. She knew all too well how true that could be. "In any case, if there's a restraining order, he's probably not allowed to see his kids or be within a certain distance of them."

"Which would explain why he might try to see them without being recognized," Meredith said slowly.

"Right. If he's caught here, there could be serious consequences, which makes the hat and sunglasses more understandable. And it would explain why he would flat-out deny being here."

"So why risk it?" Meredith asked. "If there could be serious consequences, why come at all?"

"What if you couldn't see your kids?" Julia asked. "Imagine they were just suddenly gone from your life, and you weren't allowed to see them."

"I can't even imagine." Meredith let out a breath.

"You might resort to strange behavior just to catch a glimpse of them."

"That's so sad."

"I agree."

Meredith nodded. "So the kids come here twice a week?"

"They must. He knows when they'll be here, and he comes to watch them play."

They sat still and watched for a few minutes longer, and then Meredith started to push herself up.

"Where are you going?" Julia asked.

"We can't just assume we understand what's going on, can we? We need to confirm our suspicions."

"You want to go talk to him?"

"That's the idea."

Julia saw her logic, but she hesitated. "I don't think he'll be pleased to see me."

"This is a public place. What can he do?" Meredith marched across the playground and stood directly in front of Calvin. Julia followed reluctantly behind. She couldn't read the look on his face as he looked up at Meredith.

"Calvin Corliss?" Meredith said.

"Who are you?"

"If you're just here to see your kids, you don't need to worry about me. I won't tell anyone I saw you. I'm just trying to get answers about some plants."

"Are you—" He broke off as he noticed Julia arriving to stand directly next to Meredith.

"You again. I thought I told you—"

"We think we understand why you lied," Julia said. "We think you're only here to watch your children. And like my friend Meredith said, if you're here for that, we'll walk away and leave you alone and tell no one. We're just interested in who planted those plants in the northwest section of the park."

He was looking around, as if searching for an exit. Julia knew he wouldn't risk making a scene.

"I told you yesterday, I don't know anything about plants," Calvin said.

"So what's with the tool belt?" Meredith pointed at it.

He hesitated, and then, apparently seeing no way out, said, "It's my lunch break. I have to wear the shirt, so I added the belt to look less like myself. To throw off anyone who might recognize me."

Julia didn't have the heart to tell him it hadn't worked, that Randy Torrez knew he was here and thought it was strange.

"Your ex hasn't spotted you?" Julia asked.

He laughed. "My ex isn't here. Now that she's fancy, she has a nanny to take the kids to the park for her."

"Where is the nanny?" Meredith asked.

Calvin pointed to a young woman with brown hair across the park.

"She doesn't know you?" Julia asked.

"No. And I'd like to keep it that way." He looked down at his hands. "Look, I'm not hurting anyone. This is the only way I get to see my kids since my wife shacked up with that banker. I just—"

He broke off and then took a moment to compose himself.

"If you could avoid telling anyone you saw me here, I'd be grateful."

Julia looked at Meredith, who nodded.

"Thank you, Calvin. Good luck." Julia turned and headed for the gate, and Meredith followed right behind.

When they were out of the playground area and heading back through the park, Meredith said, "That was about the saddest thing I've seen in a while."

"It's tragic to see a man so desperate to see his kids he'd resort to that level of deception," Julia agreed. "But for our purposes, I think we can cross Calvin off the suspect list."

"I suppose you're right." Meredith took off her sunglasses and used the edge of her shirt to wipe them clean. "Which leaves us with...not much."

"We've still got Angela," Julia reminded her. "I've got a good feeling about her."

"A few minutes ago, you were sure Calvin was our man."

"Well, now that I know he isn't, I'm turning my focus to Angela."

"Fair enough."

They walked back to the office, and while Meredith went into her office to finish up a few things before Chase and the kids came to pick her up, Julia turned back to Angela's YouTube videos. She didn't know if there was a way to find out anything more about her from the videos, but she was about out of ideas.

Julia sat down and started a video. Angela began explaining about aquatic or oceanic scents, which apparently were based on a synthetic chemical that gave scents a hint of salty sea breeze. Julia kept her eyes focused on the background but didn't see much. There was a pile of clothes on Angela's bed in this video, but they were gone in the next, which was about fruity scents such as mango, black currant, and passion fruit.

The camera was set up at a slightly different angle this time, and Julia could see more of the wardrobe. Aside from the missing clothes, the room looked otherwise the same. She watched video after video, hoping for something, anything, that would tell her more about Angela, but aside from learning a lot about perfume, it wasn't getting her anywhere.

Julia decided to try a few more videos before she gave up. This video was about green scents, such as cut grass, crushed green leaf, and cucumber. In this video, there were clothes draped over the door of the wardrobe. She paused the video and looked at what appeared to be a black polo shirt on top. It had some kind of white symbol on the breast.

Julia studied the image, trying to understand it. It looked like a hexagon next to a pentagon, some with sticks poking off of them. What was that? There looked to be little letters or something at some of the points. And were those zeroes? She narrowed her eyes, trying to make it come into focus, but all she saw was a strange grid of lines that didn't make any sense. Julia did a screen capture and enlarged the photo, adjusting the coloring so that the black was blacker and the white was brighter, but it still didn't make any sense.

Julia gave up on that video and watched the next one. In this shot, which had been filmed back in February, she recognized a coupon hanging on the bulletin board. It was for a local pizza place popular with students, but she didn't see how that was any use. In a video filmed in May, there was a cardboard box on the bed. Julia was bleary-eyed and growing frustrated. This was going nowhere.

She heard the front door open, and from the voices coming down the hallway she quickly surmised that Chase and the kids were here to pick up Meredith. She heard Kinsley and Kaden arguing good-naturedly about something or other.

"I think the kids are here," Julia called.

Meredith laughed. "Sounds like it."

Julia knew why Chase had wanted to come to the office to pick up Meredith. There was more than a casual flirtation between

Meredith's younger son and Carmen. He'd wanted to come by the office to see Carmen.

While Chase and Carmen chatted, the kids wandered down the hallway back toward the offices.

"Did you find the person who planted those flowers yet?" Kinsley asked, appearing in the doorway of Julia's office. She stepped inside, her brother just a step behind.

"We're working on it," Julia said.

"Looks like you're watching YouTube to me," Kinsley said, smiling. She pointed at a video Julia had paused on the screen. It was the one that had been filmed in May, with the cardboard box on the bed. Julia had been trying to make out what the writing on the side of the box said.

"I *was* watching YouTube." Julia considered how much to say but then decided that the kids had been involved in the case the whole time, so she might as well share what she was up to. "We think this might be one of the suspects we found in the video footage you helped us find."

"Who is she?"

Kinsley walked around the desk to get a better look, and Kaden followed behind her.

"Her name is Angela. She makes videos about the ingredients in perfume."

"Those sound like boring videos," Kaden said.

"They sound better than those stupid science videos you watch all the time," Kinsley said.

"Those videos are not stupid. They're a lot better than those unicorn videos you like."

"All right. Break it up, you two." Siblings never changed. "Hey, can either of you read what that says?" Julia pointed at the writing on the side of the box on the bed.

Both Kinsley and Kaden leaned in and squinted at it, but it was too small.

"Nope," Kinsley said.

"Not me," Kaden said.

"What's that picture?" Kinsley pointed to the logo on the shirt in the background of Angela's room.

"I was trying to figure out what that symbol was, but it just looks like a bunch of lines to me," Julia said.

"It kind of looks like a strange octopus," Kinsley said. "But, like, with squares."

"Okay, A, those are not squares." Kaden rolled his eyes. "They're hexagons. And B, that's the chemical structure of caffeine."

"Wait. It's what?" Julia asked.

"That's what that picture is," Kaden said. "See, that N is for nitrogen, the H is hydrogen, the O is—"

"Okay, *we get it*," Kinsley said.

"Kaden, are you sure?" Julia felt her heartbeat speed up. Caffeine was the name of a new coffee shop just off Forsyth Park. Meredith had walked by and seen that it seemed very modern and sleek inside. Was there any chance this was their logo?

"I'm sure." Kaden said it so simply and confidently that she didn't doubt it.

She opened up a browser window, typed in "Caffeine Forsyth Park," and quickly found the website. The tagline at the top of the pages read *Better coffee. Because, science.* The website explained that extensive scientific testing had helped them engineer the perfect roast and the right amount of time to froth the milk. The menu included drinks such as Molecular Mocha and Atomic Americano. Julia supposed every business needed a gimmick, and it seemed this place had decided to double down on the science angle. It didn't take a big leap of logic to guess that Angela might work at the coffee shop.

"Kaden, you may have just helped in a big way."

Kaden didn't respond in any way to the praise, but Kinsley stuck out her bottom lip.

"And Kinsley, you were very helpful too." Kinsley cheered up at that, and then Chase called from the front of the office that it was time for them to get going. The kids scampered out.

"I'm headed out with them," Meredith said.

"Wait. Before you go, check this out." Julia filled Meredith in on the discovery about the coffee shop where she guessed Angela worked.

"That kid. I don't know where he learns this stuff," Meredith said.

"Kaden is a special kid," Julia said. "And he may have just provided us with a way to get a hold of Angela."

"Wow. I assume that means you're going to pay a visit to the coffee shop soon?" Meredith hovered in the doorway. Julia could see she was torn.

"Go spend time with your family," Julia insisted. "I'll let you know if I learn anything."

"Okay," Meredith said. "Just don't have too much fun without me."

"Have a good evening. Tell Quin I said hello."

"You have a good weekend too."

Once Meredith and the kids had left, Julia decided to take a stroll over to the coffee shop. It was a short walk down Whitaker to Hall Street, one of the side streets that branched off away from the park. Julia found the coffee shop a few blocks down. The symbol that Kaden had identified at the chemical structure of caffeine was hung in the window.

The coffee shop wasn't crowded. Julia approached the dark blue plastic counter that reflected her image back at her. The side wall was covered in a huge periodic table of the elements, and Julia saw that the customers at the tables were drinking out of glass beakers.

"Welcome to Caffeine. How can I help you?" The young man behind the counter had curly brown hair and a strong jawline. He was wearing a black polo shirt with the same symbol on the breast.

"Can I please have a Chemical Cappuccino?" Julia asked.

"Boiling point or freezing point?"

"Are you asking if I want that hot or iced?"

"Exactly."

"Iced, please."

"Great. Quark, proton, or nuclear?"

"Huh?"

"Small, medium, or large?"

"Oh. Medium, please."

"That will be five seventeen," he said.

Julia handed over the money and causally asked, "Is Angela Gilkie working today?"

"Nah, she doesn't usually work Fridays."

Julia wanted to pump her fist. They'd gotten it right. Angela worked here.

"Can you tell me when she'll be in?" she asked.

"I'd have to check the schedule. I think she might be in tomorrow, but I'm not sure."

"Would you be able to give me her phone number?" Julia asked.

"Uh…" He shifted on his feet. "Who are you, exactly?"

"I'm very interested in talking with her." Julia neatly dodged the question.

"I don't think I can give out personal information for other employees," the man said.

Good for him, Julia thought. He shouldn't give out that information for safety reasons. Still, though, it would have been pretty convenient if he had.

"That's all right. I understand." Julia smiled, and after she signed for her drink using the little screen, she went down to the end of the counter and waited. A few minutes later, she was walking back to the office, sipping her drink. She decided to call Meredith to tell her the good news.

"Are you on your way to dinner?" Julia asked. She didn't want to interrupt Meredith's night out.

"Not yet. Quin is supposed to be here in about twenty minutes," Meredith said. "What did you find?"

"She works there," Julia said. "She works at Caffeine."

"Was she there?" Meredith asked. "I'll be so jealous if you got to—"

"No, she wasn't there."

"Too bad," Meredith said. "But okay. Let's say we have the right person. Say Angela is the one who planted that garden. Based on what we saw in the video footage, she shows up at the garden every other day or so. What do you think is the likelihood she comes over to the garden after she's done with work?"

Meredith considered this.

"Why wouldn't she be wearing the uniform when we saw her in the video, then?" Meredith asked.

"Maybe she changes before she leaves?" Julia suggested. "I worked in a coffee shop one summer in college, and even if you manage to keep your clothes clean working behind an espresso machine, you smell like a shot of espresso when you leave. I would change before leaving just as often as not, especially if I wasn't going straight home afterward."

"Okay. Fair enough," Meredith said. "And she looks enough like the girl in the video footage that I think it's fair to say it could be her. Plus, Angela's in the Eco Club, and she's here in Savannah for the summer. She's headed to the right part of the park in the video. She had a datura flower."

"But why?" Julia asked. "That's what I can't get my head around. What's her motive? Why would she plant those plants in the garden?"

"Remember what Maggie Lu said," Meredith said. "Don't focus on the negative. She seems so sweet in the videos. I bet there's a good reason. Maybe she just likes to garden. I bet living in a dorm she doesn't have that opportunity."

"But why those flowers? If she just likes flowers, why wouldn't she plant peonies or roses or...something normal? Why plant a whole slew of poisonous plants?"

"There were other plants there too, don't forget. And I have a theory," Meredith said.

"What's that?"

"Herbal supplements."

"Okay." Julia processed this. "You think she harvests the leaves and petals and whatnot and uses them to make herbal supplements?"

"That's my theory. Remember what it says on her YouTube channel?"

"Remind me."

"Hang on. Let me pull it up." She heard Meredith typing, and then, "It says, 'Fragrance fiend. Herbalist and nature lover. I share about my passion for how natural ingredients make the world a more lovely place.' Couldn't that bit about being an herbalist refer to herbal supplements?"

"It could," Julia had to agree. "And as Maggie Lu pointed out, the plants in that garden all have some purported health benefits. So that could make sense."

"Wait," Meredith said. "Okay, plus there's this."

"There's what?" Julia asked.

"I'm looking at a video shot in May. There's a box in the shot."

"I saw that earlier, but I couldn't read the writing on the side of the box," Julia said.

"Right. You can't see it right now. But just wait. Later in the video, you can see it more clearly."

"What?"

"The second half must have been a different take than the first part of video, because the box has moved."

"A different take? The videos are all filmed in one shot, aren't they?"

"No, if you look closely, you can see where they've been spliced together. Usually it's pretty subtle, but I did notice this. In the first half of the video, the box is at a different angle than later in the video."

"Hang on. I'm almost at the office." Julia hurried across the small yard and up the steps. She waved to Carmen as she hurried past and into her office. She set down her coffee and opened a browser window. "Okay, I'm at my desk. Let me pull it up."

"Let me know when you have it."

"Okay. I'm there."

"Go to time stamp 8:37."

"Hang on." Julia moved the bar across the bottom of the video. As Meredith had told her, the box was now on the bed. "Oh. Wow."

"In this shot, you can see that it says HERB AFFAIR on the side of the box."

"What is Herb Affair?" Julia asked.

"I'm googling it right now."

"Me too." Julia typed in the name and pulled up the first link.

"They sell empty pill capsules and supplies," Meredith said.

Julia saw that indeed, the site seemed to be entirely devoted to selling empty pill capsules and ways to fill them.

The evidence that pointed toward Angela was growing more overwhelming with each revelation.

"So if Angela is our gardener, how do we approach her?" Julia asked.

"I mean, I guess we could approach her at the coffee shop, but what are we going to do, ask her if she's guilty and hope she says yes?"

"You're right. We need to catch her in the act," Julia said. "We need photographic evidence that we can take to the police and prove she's responsible."

"So, a stakeout," Meredith said. "Assuming she's still coming to the garden now that she knows the plants have been discovered."

"Can we narrow down the time we need to have someone in the park?" Julia asked. They did plenty of stakeouts in the course of their jobs, and they were not the most interesting way to pass the time. Sitting around doing nothing sounded like it might be fun, but it could actually be excruciatingly boring. It could also be a big time waster if they ended up sitting around and Angela didn't come. And Meredith wasn't going to want to spend hours sitting around the park while the grandkids were in town.

"Let's say she comes after her shift," Meredith said. "In that case, we know she won't be coming to the park today. But she may be coming tomorrow. She was on the video footage from last Saturday, wasn't she?"

"Yes," Julia said. "Beau is playing at a charity golf tournament tomorrow. Having to do a stakeout would give me the perfect excuse to get out of that."

Meredith laughed. "Okay. I would offer to take a shift, but I'm supposed to take the kids and Chase to the beach tomorrow."

"That's okay. Enjoy your time with the kids." They would probably head to Tybee Island, a beautiful stretch of soft sand that jutted out into the ocean.

"Thank you for understanding."

"It's no problem. No sense in both of us spending all day sitting in the bushes. I'll be there," Julia said. "And I can't wait to catch her."

Chapter Seventeen

CASSIE SHOWED UP AT EIGHT on Saturday morning, just like she'd promised. She wore capri-length workout pants and a fitted tank top, and she looked lean and svelte. Julia felt ridiculous next to her in Beau's old baggy basketball shorts and a loose T-shirt.

"What do you think? Should we stay local, or should we go somewhere fun?" Cassie asked. "How much time do you have?"

"What do you mean?" Julia had already had a cup of coffee, but she wasn't following.

"I mean, running on city streets is fine, but I prefer to go somewhere a bit different. It makes it more interesting."

"I went to Lake Mayer Park the other day," Julia said.

"Right. Like that. Didn't it make your run better to have something interesting to look at?"

"Yes, it did. I mean, it was still awful, but it was slightly less awful than usual."

"So how about we do one of my favorite runs today?"

Julia hesitated. There was no telling what kind of torture Cassie had up her sleeve. Would she remember that Julia was a beginner? That it was hot out? But Julia had said she would trust her.

"Okay," Julia said. "Where to?"

"How does Fort Pulaski sound?"

"What?" Fort Pulaski was a Civil War battleground, a brick military garrison on Cockspur Island, at the mouth of the Savannah River. The Confederacy had believed the fort to be impenetrable, but the North had the new technology of rifled cannons that shot cannonballs farther and harder than the traditional cannonballs it had been built to withstand. When the North attacked, the fort crumbled, forcing the Confederate soldiers to surrender. These days, it was a national park, and visitors could still see the pockmarked surface where the cannonballs had broken through the walls. "You can run there?"

"There's a nice flat rail trail that goes along McQueen's Island, and you can cross the bridge over to Cockspur Island. There are trails that go all around the fort, including one that ends right at the tip of the island, with a great view of the lighthouse."

"That sounds like a long run."

"There's a parking lot just before the bridge. It'll be just over a mile and a half each way. So, just about the right distance if you're training for a 5K."

Julia had to admit, it did sound more appealing than running through the neighborhood again.

"Okay, I'll give it a try."

"Awesome."

"When did you take up running?" Julia asked when they were buckled in and headed toward the highway. "I know Wyatt runs, but I never knew you to run before."

"I started running when I decided it was time to finally get my head on straight," Cassie said. "I discovered it helped me relax."

Julia snorted.

"I mean, obviously the running part itself is not relaxing," Cassie said. "But it gives me time to just be in my head, with no distractions, and my mind always feels clearer when I'm done. And my body is exhausted, which means I'm more peaceful the rest of the day."

"I haven't gotten to that point yet."

"I hope you do. But maybe running isn't your thing. That's okay. It's just something that has helped me. And I'm grateful that you're willing to try it."

"I'm glad." She could actually see what Cassie was talking about. Her sister did seem calmer, somehow, now that Julia took the time to notice.

"I'll never be a marathon runner or anything." Cassie smiled. "And I'm slow. But that's okay with me. I just like to get out and get some exercise and explore cool places I wouldn't see otherwise, and the mental health benefits are unbeatable."

They turned onto McQueen's Island, a narrow strip of land that stood between salt marshes and the southern branch of the Savannah River. Julia smelled the tang of the sea air over the marsh as they drove along a small highway and parked in a gravel lot.

"Down that way is the rail trail," Cassie said, pointing down a path covered with crushed rocks. "It goes to the western tip of the island. But we'll head this way." She pointed to the low bridge that crossed the channel to Cockspur Island.

Julia stretched for a minute and then said, "All right. I'm ready when you are."

Cassie started off with a slow jog down the side of the road, and Julia was able to keep up. It was pretty, she had to admit. There were salt marshes all around them. The tide must be high, because they were flooded with a briny water that smelled like nothing else in the world. But it was hot, and the air was sticky.

They got to the bridge, a narrow causeway that had only a small strip of pavement at the side for a sidewalk, but as the park wasn't open yet, there was no traffic. Julia's legs were tight and rebelled against the movement, and her breath started coming harder. But the river glistened in the sun; tiny golden specks of sunlight danced as the water flowed to the sea beneath them.

Julia was breathing even harder by the time they made it to the other side and stepped onto Cockspur Island, and Cassie slowed her pace. From here, the battered fort loomed, each cannonball blast in its scarred sides a sad reminder of the hubris that had led the Confederacy to believe it could not fall. Julia followed Cassie as she led them along the road, but it rose steadily in a long uphill toward the fort, and Julia couldn't take it.

"Hang on." She stopped and leaned forward to catch her breath.

"No problem." Cassie didn't even look winded.

Julia eyed the long incline in front of them.

"I don't know about this. Is there another way?"

Cassie didn't answer immediately. Then she said, "Even if there was, I wouldn't want to take it. I know you can do this, Jules, just like you've accomplished everything you ever put your mind to."

Julia was too winded to answer.

"Remember when we were kids, and we decided we wanted to go off the high dive at the pool? We said we were going to do it all summer, but we were too scared until the last week of summer. I chickened out, but you made up your mind you were going to just do it. And so you did."

Julia nodded.

"And then you went off it again and again and again until Mom dragged us home, because you realized it was actually really fun."

"This is hardly the same thing," Julia managed to say.

"Well, no. But I was so impressed that you made up your mind you were going to do something and you did it. That's how you've always approached life. I mean, you went off to college when everyone, including me, thought you should marry that guy you were dating and settle down. What was his name?"

"Gary," she said. Her breath was starting to slow, but it was still hard to talk.

"Right. But you wanted to get a degree, so you did. And then a law degree. You were one of, what, twenty women in your law school class?"

Julia nodded.

"You decided you wanted to help families, and so you went out and did it like it was nothing. Of course you did, because that's how you do everything. You just make up your mind and do it. I've always wished I were more like you in that way."

Julia didn't speak, but this time it wasn't because she couldn't. She didn't know what to say.

"I don't mean to make this a big deal. I just mean that I know you can do this, just like you've done every other thing you ever decided you wanted to do. You don't need to worry about me. I'm all in. Just make up your mind you're going to do it, and no one will be able to stop you."

Was that all it would take? Shifting her focus from Cassie to deciding she would do this crazy thing? Julia didn't know. But she did know that on some level Cassie was right. Julia was good at accomplishing whatever she put her mind to. So she decided to try.

I'm going to run this 5K, she decided, and then, before she could change her mind, she took off running. Cassie laughed and caught up to run alongside her. Cassie directed them up the hill and around the fort and then down a narrow path that wound through brambles and boxwood bushes. *Nature*, Julia thought. Running could get you out into nature.

They followed the path until it ended, at the southern tip of the island. And there, across another narrow channel, rose the Cockspur Island Lighthouse, a squat, battered white brick light that stood out in the harbor. Julia knew that it hadn't been operational in over a hundred years, but there it stood, strong and proud and beautiful, a symbol of safety for miles around.

"It's so beautiful," Cassie said, using the edge of her shirt to wipe sweat from her brow.

It was pretty, standing out there surrounded by water dappled with the sun. And Julia wouldn't be here this morning if not for her sister's harebrained idea. Despite the pain in her lungs and in her side and in her legs, Julia was glad to be here to see it. She was glad to be here with Cassie. She looked over at her little sister and smiled.

"Ready to keep going?" Julia asked.

Cassie nodded, and they turned around and ran back up the path together.

***

Julia figured she was hours early, but she made her way to the hidden garden in Forsyth Park just after noon, well before she expected

Angela to show up—if she showed up. The past two Saturdays, she'd entered the park around four, after, Julia guessed, her shift at the coffee shop. She was hoping Angela would keep to the same pattern today.

After her run, Julia had invited Cassie to stay for breakfast, and Beau had made them omelets and hash browns. After Cassie left, Julia had showered and done chores around the house while Beau got ready for his golf tournament. She'd also called Randy Torrez and told him what she was planning to do, and he promised to be nearby in case she needed him. Then she'd packed a bag full of supplies and headed to the park. She climbed the fence and found a spot where she could be mostly hidden by one of the azalea bushes, but she could still see out and have a good camera angle. From here she should be able to get plenty of photos and even video footage of Angela tending to her plants.

Julia looked toward the flowers. The caution tape had been removed again. It sat in a ball on the far side of the small open area. Angela had been back.

Julia was struck once again by how beautiful the flowers were, blooming in the dappled sunlight. Datura was still one of the most stunning flowers she'd ever seen, and the stems heavy with monkshood and angel's-trumpet were such a gorgeous deep shade of blue. The small crimson berries of the belladonna plant glistened in the light, their skins taut and shiny and so attractive. Now that she knew what the plants were, she knew to stay away from them. How ironic that something so beautiful could be so deadly.

But the plants had good properties too. They were likely being harvested for their benefits, after all. And there were the smaller echinacea and peppermint planted right alongside them. The good mixed in with the bad. Not all one or the other but both at the same time. Complicated. Like people, she supposed. Each one different, every one composed of good qualities and not-so-good, things they'd like to forget and ways they were striving to overcome them and change their future.

Julia pulled a book out of her bag and started to read. Meredith liked to do crossword puzzles while she was in the field, while Julia had developed a taste for reading mysteries. The only problem came when she sometimes found herself so engrossed in the story that she didn't notice whatever it was she was supposed to be paying attention to.

Today she was reading a mystery about an archaeologist on the coast of England who had found a body in the salt marsh around her home. The description of the setting made Julia think about the salt marsh she and Cassie had seen on their run this morning, the strange stillness that settled over a place that was part land and part sea. Neither one nor the other but both at the same time. In her book, the heroine was busy talking to the neighbors and using her knowledge of the ancient civilizations that had occupied the land thousands of years ago to make sense of several early modern tools found near the body. Julia lost herself in the story.

About an hour into the stakeout, her phone buzzed, and she looked down to find a message from Carmen. CONFIRMED: ANGELA IS WORKING AT CAFFEINE. Julia texted back, THANKS! She'd felt bad asking Carmen to help with work on a Saturday, but Carmen had been excited to help. She'd agreed to duck into the coffee shop and see if Angela was working. If she wasn't, Julia wasn't sure whether it was worth it to keep hiding. But with Carmen's confirmation, Julia was glad to stay and wait. If they were right that Angela came by the garden after her shift, then Julia was wasting her time now, since she was clearly at work, and in the video, she hadn't come past the security camera until after four. But in case Angela did something different today, she would be here waiting.

Off in the distance, Julia heard children shrieking and dogs barking, and she overheard snippets of conversations as people walked past, completely unaware of the small hidden garden just beyond the bushes. All in all, it wasn't a bad way to spend an afternoon, sitting in the shade in a park reading a book. It would be better if there weren't azalea branches in her face and poking into her back, and her sore leg muscles were starting to cramp up, but she didn't dare move out of her spot and risk scaring Angela away. Still, it beat many other lines of work, Julia decided.

A few hours into the stakeout, she'd not seen a soul and her stomach was grumbling. She reached into her bag and pulled out a protein bar and a Diet Dr Pepper. Essential fuel for a stakeout. She read as she enjoyed her snack, and then looked down when another text message came in.

How's it going? Meredith asked.

No sign of her yet, Julia texted back. How's the beach?

Awful. You would hate it. She sent a picture of her toes in the sand, the kids splashing in the waves in front of her.

Julia was glad Meredith was having a good time. She deserved it.

As four o'clock neared, Julia set her book aside. She had her phone at the ready to capture pictures and video footage of Angela checking on the garden. Still she waited. As the clock edged toward four thirty, she started to worry that Angela wasn't coming today after all, that this whole thing had been a waste of time.

But then, just as Julia was starting to lose hope, she heard footsteps coming down the path toward her. She'd heard other footsteps throughout the afternoon, but those had belonged to couples murmuring quietly or children running, chased by harried parents. None were as purposeful and direct as these steps were. Julia pressed the RECORD button, and the camera began filming. There was a rustling of the bushes just behind Julia, and then, a few moments later, there she was. Angela. Her face was shaded by the same floppy hat, and she wore sunglasses, but it was definitely her. She wore a white T-shirt and carried that same cloth bag over her shoulder, and she had earbuds in her ears.

Julia quickly sent Randy Torrez a text: SHE'S IN THE GARDEN.

Julia watched as Angela set the bag on the ground and knelt in front of the bed of plants. Oh dear. Angela had picked a perfect spot to block the view of what she was doing. Julia saw her pull pruning shears out of the bag, but she couldn't see her actually cutting the plants. Would the video be enough if you couldn't see her actually gathering the flowers and leaves? Julia hoped so. But then again, it wasn't possible to actually see who she was in this footage. Because Angela's back was to the camera and because of the hat and the glasses, she couldn't be positively identified, even though Julia was sure it was her. Unfortunately, that meant plausible deniability. And if the footage couldn't prove who she was... Well, this video was going to be no good for anything.

Julia would have to find a better position. She hoped the earbuds meant Angela was listening to something that would cover any noise Julia was about to make. She left the bench, hunched over, and crept slowly, quietly to the side, edging her way out of the bush. If she could just get a little more to the left, she would be able to get a clearer shot. Then, carefully, she straightened up, and a branch of the bush snapped back.

Julia knew it the moment Angela heard her. Angela froze, and her shoulders tensed up. She stopped what she was doing—cutting leaves off the echinacea plant, it turned out—and turned slowly. There was nowhere for Julia to go, not quickly enough to disappear, anyway. Julia's heart was pounding and blood was rushing in her ears, but she tried to think quickly. The camera was still recording, so she decided to go on the offensive.

"What are you doing?" Julia asked.

"Who are you?" Angela's voice was familiar after Julia had seen so many of her videos. She set down the pruning shears and looked up at Julia. Her eyes were covered by the sunglasses, but her posture was defensive, tense.

"I know who you are, Angela," Julia said as calmly as she could. "I just want to know what you're doing."

"It's none of your business." Angela pushed herself up to standing, and she moved toward Julia. "Put that phone down. Are you recording me?"

"I wanted proof that you were the one who planted this garden," Julia said, again keeping her voice as calm as she could. "And now I want to know why. Did you plant this garden to make your herbal supplements?"

"Who are you? What are you even doing here?"

"I'm the person who found your secret garden and is trying to understand why you planted poisonous plants in a public park."

"You don't know that it was me."

"I know that you're the one who comes here several times a week after your shift at the coffee shop to tend to the plants and harvest their leaves and flowers for your herbal supplement business."

Angela reared her head back. "What are you, some kind of spy? Do you know how creepy that is?"

"I'm a private investigator, and I'm trying to understand why you chose a public park for your private herb garden."

Angela lifted her chin. "I'm not doing anything wrong."

"That's debatable."

"I pay taxes. Why shouldn't I use this place like everyone else?"

"Most people who use the park play basketball or enjoy the playground. Most don't cultivate their own private garden."

"I live in a dorm. What am I supposed to do?" Disdain colored Angela's words. "I don't have a place to grow them at the dorm."

"So you planted them here, in a public park."

"What? Like I said, I pay taxes. I don't care about basketball or playgrounds or whatever else you think I should be doing here. I needed dirt, and I found it. It's not a crime to grow your own plants."

Julia held back a smile. There it was—the confession she had been looking for.

"But this is a public park. You can't just plant your own garden here. And some of the plants you put in your own private garden are known to be poisonous. You have plants that can kill someone if they stumble across them. Why would you grow plants like these where someone could unknowingly get hurt or even killed?"

Angela put her hands on her hips. "Why do you think I planted them back here, where no one would find them? No one is supposed to be back here. How did you even find this place?"

"But I did find it." Julia didn't bother to answer her question—that she'd seen movement back behind the bushes, and it had probably been Angela herself that had brought attention to this little plot of land. "And I know of several dogs that have gotten sick after coming back here."

"Is that what ate my jimson weed?" Angela shook her head. "Do you know how hard that stuff is to grow?"

Julia wasn't sure how to respond. She didn't know what she'd expected—remorse, apologies, concern of some kind. But Angela didn't seem to feel any of those emotions. She simply seemed annoyed that her plants had been disturbed. How could she not care that she'd put people at risk?

"Look, I found a spot where I thought it was safe, okay? I need these plants."

"For your herbal supplements business."

"For *my mom*."

Julia had not been expecting that. "What?"

"Oh, suddenly you don't know something about my life," Angela sneered. "The reason I'm growing these plants is that my mom has Parkinson's."

"Your mom?" Julia felt a punch to her gut. Her grandfather had suffered from Parkinson's disease in his later years. The shaking and tremors and loss of control over his body had been even harder than the dementia that accompanied it. Watching his slow decline had been excruciating.

SAVANNAH SECRETS

"Yeah, apparently it's not just a disease old people get. Turns out it can affect people in their forties, and Mom is one of the lucky ones."

"I'm so sorry." Seeing her grandfather suffer from the terrible disease had been hard. She couldn't imagine what it must be like to see someone much younger—Angela's own mother—suffer from it.

"Yeah, it's terrible. But in one of her support groups, they recommended several kinds of herbal therapies, like turmeric and belladonna."

Julia remembered reading that Parkinson's disease had been listed as one of the conditions belladonna had been said to treat.

"Turmeric is easy enough to come by," Angela continued. "But we found the belladonna supplements online were pretty weak. Someone in her groups had tried it fresh, though, and it worked much better. Mom lives in an apartment and can't grow it, so I decided to grow it myself, and lo and behold, it helps a lot."

Julia felt some of her indignation vanish. Angela had been growing these plants to help her mom?

"But what about the other plants you have here? Surely they're not here to help your mother?"

"Once I started doing research on it, I discovered that all kinds of plants are used to help people. So I decided to grow all kinds of plants."

Maggie Lu's words came back to her now. Most things weren't all good or all bad. Even the selfish, reckless act of planting this garden had been motivated by good intentions, at least at first. Most people had both good and bad mixed up together, and you couldn't judge someone by one aspect of what they did. People were more complicated than that. She supposed the same was true of these plants, in the end. Sure, some of the specimens in this garden could kill. But those same plants could also help someone who was suffering from a terrible disease.

It didn't change that what Angela had done was wrong, of course. It had been reckless and foolish and completely against the rules of the park, if not the law. But now that Julia understood why Angela had done it, she felt she couldn't be as angry about it as she had been. She even kind of understood how in a teenager's twisted logic, the end justified the means.

The bushes began to rustle again, and a moment later, Randy Torrez stepped into the hidden garden. Julia watched as Angela registered the parks department polo.

"This is the girl who caused all this trouble, huh?" Randy appraised her.

"And you must be the one who keeps trying to ruin my garden."

Julia wasn't sure what would happen to Angela now. She was pretty sure the garden would be destroyed—at least the dangerous plants would be removed—and she didn't know what consequences Angela would face for her actions. Julia was surprised to realize that she hoped for leniency for Angela. She'd done a very stupid thing for a very good reason. Like most things, her actions were more complicated than they seemed. This garden had both good and bad, planted right there next to each other.

Chapter Eighteen

THE LATE JUNE DAY HAD dawned cooler than expected, and as Julia stretched, reaching for her toes, she found herself not nearly as nervous as she thought she would be. Runners milled around in nylon shorts and breathable shirts. Some wore T-shirts from Washington Elementary School. Families had signed up to run together, she saw, and some were even pushing strollers.

Wyatt was here, already lining up near the start line with the other runners who seemed to be taking this seriously in their high-end gear. She couldn't see him through the crowd, but he'd given her a hug and thanked her for being here before he went off to get a good starting position. Most of the rest of the crowd seemed much more relaxed, here to support the school more than to record a winning time.

"How are you doing?" Cassie asked. She rested her hand on Julia's shoulder, bracing herself as she pulled on her ankle to stretch the front of her thigh.

"I'm doing all right." Julia was surprised to realize that she meant it. She felt pretty good. In the past three weeks, she'd run 3.1 miles—the length of the race today—more than half a dozen times. She found that she wasn't worried about whether she could do this. She knew that she could. "You?"

"I'm great." Cassie gave her a grin and a thumbs-up. "It looks like the mere mortals are starting to line up." She nodded toward the street, where the rest of the crowd was starting to settle in behind the more serious runners at the front. "Shall we?"

"I guess we should." Together, Julia and Cassie walked across the parking lot of the elementary school toward the gathering crowd. Together. Part of Julia couldn't believe that she and Cassie were here like this. That Cassie had done exactly what she'd promised she would, and helped Julia get ready for this day. That they were lining up side by side to run this race. A year ago, Julia never would have believed it possible, and yet, here they were. Maybe Cassie really had changed, Julia began to realize. Maybe she truly was trying to be a part of their lives again. And maybe Julia herself needed to change the lens she used to view her sister, to see her for who she was now, not who she had been in the past.

An announcer began talking over the PA system, welcoming the runners and families and thanking them for raising money for the school. "Because of your hard work, we're thrilled to announce that we have raised enough money to not only fix the air-conditioning, but also give the boys' bathroom a much-needed overhaul," he announced. The crowd roared, and Julia felt goose bumps rise up on her arms. They'd done this. All these people here who had gathered pledges, one dollar at a time, had actually raised enough money to accomplish more than the goal they had set out to do.

"We're going to get started in just a few minutes here, but first I wanted to thank our sponsors," the announcer continued.

Julia turned to Cassie while he droned on. "You don't need to stay with me on the course," she said. "I know you're a lot faster than I am. Go ahead and run at your own pace."

Cassie grinned. "You can't get rid of me that easily. I said we'd do this together, and I meant it. I'll be beside you, every step of the way."

Julia knew that Cassie was only talking about the race they were about to run. She was only promising that she wouldn't abandon Julia to earn a faster finishing time. But part of Julia couldn't help but think that she meant a whole lot more.

"And now Isabella Mendez, a fourth grader here at Washington Elementary, will sing the National Anthem," the announcer said. He handed the mic to a girl in a formal pink dress and shiny shoes, and she began to sing.

"She's good," Cassie said as Isabella began to belt out the song.

"She really is," Julia agreed. The girl had an easy confidence, and she performed naturally. They listened as the young girl nailed every bar of the challenging tune. The crowd erupted into a roar as she hit the high notes at the end. And then, before Julia knew what was happening, a starting gun went off, and the crowd around her started moving.

"Let's go." Cassie held out her hand for a fist bump, and Julia returned it, and they started to jog.

Julia hadn't anticipated how crowded it would be or that she wouldn't have been able to break into a full-out run even if she'd wanted to. There were too many people running in too narrow a space for any of them to go very fast.

"It'll thin out," Cassie promised, and as they ran through the streets of the quaint neighborhood, Julia realized she was right. By the time they'd made it to the half-mile mark, they were able to spread out a bit more, and Julia settled into a steady pace. Some people passed them, and some fell behind, but she and Cassie ran together.

"There's water up ahead," Cassie said, pointing to a table set up under a sign that said MILE 1. Cups were stacked neatly on the table, but Julia realized that she didn't need any water yet. She shook her head, and she and Cassie kept running.

Residents of the neighborhood stood out on their front lawns to cheer as they went by, and several had set up sprinklers to spray into the road so runners could cool off. Julia hadn't realized how many people would be here cheering them on. It felt special to be a part of something that brought so many people out to help their community.

The course had been mostly flat, but as they neared the second mile marker, the road began to rise, and Julia felt her lungs begin to burn.

"You can do this," Cassie said. "Just past this hill, there's a long downhill."

Julia pushed through, and she found that Cassie was right. Once they started back down the hill, she felt gravity pull her forward, and they went faster as they covered the course, one step at a time.

"Anna Beth and the girls said they would be waiting just around that turn," Cassie said, pointing to a curve in the road after the stoplight. Julia looked for them as the sisters neared, and she was still some distance away when she saw Beau and Anna Beth and heard Kennedy and Madison screaming, "Go Nana! Go Grandma! Go Nana!" They were jumping up and down and clapping as Julia and Cassie ran past, and Julia felt a surge of something she hadn't expected. Love, sure, and tenderness, but also excitement. Her girls were watching. Her girls were seeing her do this. Would they believe that they could do it too?

The thought filled her with pride, and with a half mile to go, a rush of adrenaline filled her, and she began to run faster. Cassie quickly adjusted her pace to match, and they ran, side by side, until they neared the third mile marker, and the finish line loomed.

That's when Julia began to sprint. The last leg of the course was lined with people cheering, shouting for her as she raced toward the finish line. She heard the wind whistle past her, and her legs and lungs were burning. But she just kept running and didn't stop until she and Cassie entered the finishing chute and crossed the finish line, with the crowd cheering all around them.

It hit her after she'd been ushered through the chute and out of the way of runners coming in behind them. Her legs felt like rubber, and she had to gasp to pull air into her lungs. Everything hurt, and she was sure she'd never breathe normally again.

"Just walk it out," Cassie said. "Keep moving. You'll recover faster that way."

So Julia kept walking, putting one foot in front of the other as her breathing slowly returned to normal and her legs began to feel solid underneath her again.

"You did it." Cassie was grinning.

Julia realized Cassie was right. She had accomplished something that had felt impossible just a few weeks ago. She had worked hard, and she had done it.

But she hadn't done it alone. "*We* did it."

And, she had to admit, she hadn't hated every moment of it. It had actually been kind of fun, if she was honest. Sure, it had been painful, but also beautiful in its own way. Good and bad, all mixed up together.

Cassie leaned forward and pulled Julia into a hug, and Julia let her arms reach around and pull her sister tight. The best part of all of this was that Cassie had been there right by her side, just as she'd promised she would be.

And Julia had the feeling she'd be there for a good long while.

Dear Reader,

This story began, as so many of them do, with a totally random interaction in my everyday life. My eight-year-old daughter was home sick from school, and after lunch she was feeling well enough to play the board game Clue.

It turns out that in the newer version of the game, they've replaced the character Mrs. White with a new character named Dr. Orchid. When I first saw this, I was upset—how could they ruin my childhood like that?! But my daughter calmly read out the short character sketch on the box—did you know the characters all have backstories? You learn something new every day, and it turns out that Dr. Orchid has a PhD in plant toxicology. She also attended boarding school in Switzerland until she was kicked out for "a near-fatal daffodil poisoning incident."

"You can poison someone with daffodils?" my daughter asked. I had never heard of such a thing, so obviously we researched that, which led to a deep dive into poisonous plants, and, well, here we are. You never know where the idea for a story is going to come from. I'm not much of a gardener myself, but I loved learning about the history and uses of so many different kinds of plants.

And ever since this group of authors started working on a series set in Savannah, the birthplace of Juliette Gordon Low, I knew I wanted to find a way to include the history of Girl Scouts in a story. I co-lead a Girl Scout troop, and I was really interested in the history of the organization, which makes a positive difference in the lives of millions of girls around the country. I found an early handbook online, and I kept emailing my co-leaders: *Did you know the first Girl Scouts earned badges for clerkship and cooking for invalids? And for knowing how to milk a cow and housekeeping?!*

Today, our girls earn badges for things like building robots and coding and entrepreneurial skills. We sell cookies to raise money for organizations and projects the kids care about, and they choose activities they think will help improve our community. But they also learn about first aid and camping and hiking and caring for others, just like the earliest Scouts did. The Victory Gardens the Scouts planted during World War I? Those are real. From the beginning, the Scouts has been about teaching girls skills that will improve their lives and expose them to new things and allow them to give back to their communities, and I had fun exploring how that was true even in its very earliest days.

I hope you enjoyed reading this book as much as I enjoyed writing it.

Beth Adams

About the Author

BETH ADAMS LIVES IN BROOKLYN, New York, with her husband and two young daughters. When she's not writing, she spends her time cleaning up after two devious cats and trying to find time to read mysteries.

The Truth Behind the Fiction

JULIETTE GORDON LOW, THE FOUNDER of Girl Scouts, was born in Savannah in 1860. Her parents, William Washington Gordon II and Eleanor "Nellie" Kinzie Gordon were well-to-do, and her father fought for the Confederacy during the Civil War. The family relocated to Chicago, where her mother's family was from, after Savannah was captured by Union troops. They returned to Savannah after the war. Juliette—nicknamed Daisy by a doting uncle—was sent to boarding school and finishing school and studied painting in New York.

She returned to Savannah after the death of her sister Alice in 1880, met William Mackay Low, and they began courting. They married in 1886. The couple lived in England and Scotland much of the time, but the marriage was not ultimately happy. They spent much of their time separated until William died in 1905.

In 1911, Juliette met Sir Robert Baden-Powell, founder of the Boy Scouts, and was inspired by the program he designed. She became involved in the British Girl Guides and started a Girl Guides group near her home in Scotland. In 1912, she returned to Savannah hoping to spread the Girl Guides to her hometown. The initial group of Girl Guides in the United States was only eighteen strong, but the movement grew quickly, largely due to Low's extensive social connections. Low renamed it the Girl Scouts shortly thereafter.

Today, Juliette Gordon Low's birthplace, on the corner of Bull Street and East Oglethorpe Avenue, is one of the most popular tourist attractions in Savannah and is visited by thousands of Girl Scouts and their families and troop leaders every year.

JULIA'S (NOT-POISONOUS) STRAWBERRY RHUBARB CRISP

Ingredients:

4 cups fresh rhubarb (about four stalks), cut into one-inch chunks

5 cups fresh strawberries, halved

1 cup sugar, divided

Zest from one orange

1 tablespoon cornstarch

½ cup orange juice (best if fresh squeezed)

1 cup flour

½ brown sugar

½ teaspoon salt

1 cup quick-cooking (not instant) oatmeal

12 tablespoons cold butter

Directions:

Preheat oven to 350. In a large bowl, toss the rhubarb, strawberries, ½ cup sugar, and orange zest. In a small bowl, dissolve the cornstarch in the orange juice and add to the fruit. Toss to coat. Pour mixture into large baking dish. You may want to set this on a baking pan to collect any juice that runs over during cooking.

To make topping, combine flour, remaining sugar, brown sugar, salt, and oatmeal in the bowl of a mixer fitted with a paddle attachment. With mixer on low speed, add butter in chunks and mix until mixture is in crumbles.

Sprinkle topping over fruit and bake for one hour, or until mixture is bubbling and topping is golden brown.

Read on for a sneak peek of another exciting book
in the Savannah Secrets!

Meant for Good

By DeAnna Julie Dodson

MEREDITH BELLEFONTAINE HURRIED UP TO the offices of Magnolia Investigations, already sweating in Savannah's July heat. She never knew whether having a Monday holiday was a blessing or a curse. The Fourth had been on Sunday, making yesterday "Independence Day Observed," and she'd enjoyed two days of grilling and fireworks and spending time with friends and family.

Now, though, she was running behind, finding as always that the more she hurried the further behind she fell. She was supposed to meet a new client at nine. It was 8:57. Carmen Lopez, the agency's assistant, would already be there, of course, but Meredith hated to rush in when a client was waiting.

Her phone rang just as she got to the door. She noticed it was her business partner, Julia Foley, so she stopped where she was to answer it.

"Mere!" Julia said breathlessly before Meredith could even say hello. "I'm sorry, but my car overheated and I had to drop it off at the garage. Now I'm driving Beau's. I should be at the office soon. If the client's already there, go ahead without me. You can fill me in when I get there."

"Okay," Meredith said when Julia finally took a breath. "I'll take care of it. You be careful. See you in a little while."

"Thanks for seeing to everything." Julia sighed. "I hate to be late."

"Not a problem. See you soon."

Meredith ended the call and took a deep breath before she opened the door and stepped into the cool hallway. She hated to have to be "on" the minute she stepped into the office. A few minutes to get settled, to get her humidity-frizzled hair back into some kind of order would be nice, but it was 8:59 now. Maybe the client was late.

"Good morning," Carmen said as Meredith peeped into the reception area. Carmen had on a flattering navy skirt and a white blouse, and there was a red headband in her glossy black hair. Her earrings were a spray of red, white, and blue sparkles. "Mrs. Cooper is here."

"Mrs. Cooper," Meredith said, smiling and extending her hand. "I'm sorry to have kept you waiting."

"Oh no." The woman shifted her purse to her left arm so she could shake hands with Meredith. "You're right on time."

"I'm Meredith Bellefontaine. My office is across the hall. We can talk there."

"Thank you. And, please, call me Lydia."

"All right. Would you like some coffee, Lydia?"

"Thank you, but I've had a cup already this morning. More than that doesn't agree with me. But, please, you go ahead."

Meredith led Lydia across the hall and settled her in the chair in front of her desk. "Give me just a minute. Thanks."

She walked back into the reception area. "Julia called. She's running a little late, but she'll be here soon."

Carmen nodded. "Okay. You don't have any messages yet."

"Good. Thanks."

Meredith got herself some coffee and then went back into her office and shut the door. She didn't know much about this case yet, and over the long weekend she had forgotten most of what she had read. But thanks to Carmen's awesome efficiency, the file for it was already on her desk. She flipped it open as she sat down.

"I understand you want us to investigate a theft," she said, smiling at Lydia.

Lydia was still clutching her large black purse, looking as if she didn't quite know what to do in a private investigator's office. Probably in her late fifties, she was bright-eyed in her preppy, black-rimmed glasses, and pleasantly plump. There was determination in her firm mouth, a determination that had obviously overcome her shyness.

"Yes. Since it's not a recent theft, it might be a little bit hard for you to find out anything at this point, but I'm hoping you can find out more than I've been able to."

"That's our specialty," Meredith said.

"That's what I was told." Lydia opened her purse and took out a newspaper article. "Your assistant said you and your partner saw this last week. As it says, I was trying to get some information about what happened when my great-grandfather was sent to prison for theft. The online group I was talking to said you might be able to help me."

Meredith took the article from her, skimmed it, and handed it back. "And how did this end up in the newspaper?"

"One of the members of the group writes human interest and local history articles. She's always on the lookout for something she thinks will make a good story." Lydia smiled shyly. "She says she wants to write a follow-up article about it when I find out what really happened."

"I hope we can do that. Do you know when this theft took place? The article isn't very clear."

"I'm not sure of an exact date, but it was in 1918, maybe September or October."

"That was certainly a while back."

Lydia nodded. "Is it too long ago for you to look into?"

"No, of course not. We've done several historical investigations. Please, tell me what you know about this theft."

"I'm sorry to say it's not a whole lot. Dale, he's my husband, says it's way too late to find out anything, but I figured a real private detective agency would have ways to find out things that regular people don't, right?"

Meredith couldn't help smiling at her eagerness. "We've learned a thing or two since we've opened."

"Well, anyway, my mother, Sheila Bryleigh, is in a memory care home."

"Oh, I'm sorry," Meredith murmured.

"It's a nice place, it really is, but it's so awful for her to be losing her memory like that. But here's what made me come to you. A few weeks ago, she started saying that Matt Van Orden wrote her a letter."

"I saw that in the article about you and your mother. But I don't know enough yet about the Van Ordens to know how that figures into anything."

Lydia winced apologetically. "I'd better start at the very beginning. My great-grandfather, Mother's grandfather, was named James Brandon. He worked for Van Orden Munitions & Manufacturing during World War I and before then."

"And Matt Van Orden was the owner of the company?" Meredith asked, taking notes.

"No, that was his father, Thomas. From what I've found out, the company did a lot of work for the government, mostly in supplying things for the army. My great-grandfather worked for Thomas Van Orden from when he started as an errand boy in 1903 until 1918. He was basically Mr. Van Orden's right-hand man by then. I had always been told by my mother and grandmother that even though he didn't have any official title in the company, he took care of Mr. Van Orden and handled pretty much anything he needed done."

"I see. And 1918 was when he was sent to prison for theft."

"Mr. Van Orden had a very valuable jewel collection. He had inherited several expensive pieces that he gave to his wife at the time of their marriage and afterward, and he bought several more too. And after she died when their son was born, he kept the jewels locked up in his safe."

"And he blamed your great-grandfather for the theft."

"Yes. My grandmother, his daughter, was eleven at the time, but I remember her telling me what it was like when the police came and arrested him. Her mother had died the year before, and my grandmother had to be taken to a neighbor's house until one of her aunts could come get her."

"So why did he think your great-grandfather was guilty? Did he have the combination to the safe?"

Lydia shook her head. "Not according to my grandmother. She told me her father always said that Mr. Van Orden was very secretive about that safe combination. He didn't think anybody could get into the safe but Mr. Van Orden himself, but the prosecutor convinced the jury that since my great-grandfather had access to Mr. Van Orden's private office and knew where the safe was, he could have figured out the combination over time by getting a glimpse of his boss opening the safe over the years and piecing together what he saw."

"That seems like it would be very hard to do."

"I think it would be almost impossible," Lydia said, "but I guess it could be done if someone was patient and observant enough. That wasn't what really hurt him at the trial though."

"What did?" Meredith flipped to a new page in her notepad and kept writing.

"Evidently he was sort of lost after his wife died. Grandma was still a little girl, like I said, and she really wasn't in a position to help him get through it. She said he drank a lot, and he got himself into trouble with gambling debts. The prosecutor found out about that and brought it out at the trial. Back then, that was about enough to convict a man of nearly anything."

"So he was sent to prison."

Lydia nodded. "He was sentenced to twenty years. He served nineteen, and then he died there."

"I'm sorry."

"He died nearly twenty-five years before I was born, so I really don't know that much about him. Just what my grandmother said about him. My mother was six when he died and never met him, but she still felt the shame of what happened to him. Of what happened to her mother because of him. My grandmother was passed from relative to relative until she was old enough to get work to support herself, but even after she married and had a new name, people would find out that her father was in prison and distance themselves from her."

"That must have been so hard for her," Meredith said, still writing as quickly as she could.

"My mother never even met her grandfather, but some parents wouldn't let her play with their children. I don't know if they thought she was going to steal their toys or what."

There was hurt in Lydia's eyes, bitterness in her words, pain for the mother and grandmother she obviously loved.

"Are you sure you wouldn't like some coffee?" Meredith asked her after a moment. Sometimes it helped to take a little break when a client was having a hard time.

Lydia took a deep breath. "No. Really, it's all right. I didn't expect to get all emotional about this. My great-grandfather died a long time ago. My grandmother passed away when I was in my teens, but she lived with us after Grandpa died. I heard all the stories about her father and about how hard it was for her and Mom because of what happened to him. I've always felt bad for Mom because I can tell she still feels like she's somehow less than everybody else. And now—" She blinked hard, obviously fighting tears. "Now she's telling me that Matt Van Orden wrote her a letter."

"Could he have?" Meredith asked. "How old would he be now?"

Lydia sniffled and blinked again. "I looked it up not long ago. He was born in 1898."

"So he'd be over one hundred and twenty."

"Yes. But that doesn't matter anyway, because he died in 1918. When he was in the navy during World War I."

"Your mother wasn't even born by then, right?"

"Right. He couldn't have sent her a letter. I asked Mom's doctor about it, and he said it's possible that she's imagined that he sent her a letter because, in her mind, she needed to have some closure about everything that happened to her family once her grandfather was sent to prison."

"Does she say when Matt sent her this letter?"

"No," Lydia said with a sigh. "She says she doesn't remember but that she knows he did and that she kept it because it was important."

"But you haven't found anything like that?"

"No. And I've looked. I thought maybe it could have been from someone in the Van Orden family or something, and Mom was only confused about it, but I haven't found anything at all from anybody about the case. Certainly nothing from anyone named Van Orden."

Meredith tapped her pencil on her notepad, thinking. "Could she tell you anything about what was in the letter? What did she say about it?"

"All she's told me is that it says her grandfather was innocent and shouldn't have gone to jail. She said too that the Van Ordens knew all along what was going on."

"What was going on about what?"

"I don't know. If I ask her, she gets confused." Lydia grimaced. "I know that's no help, but I guess that kind of backs up what the doctor said about her wanting some closure about what happened to her and her mother."

"Is your mother aware of what's going on around her?" Meredith asked as gently as she was able. "Does she recognize you?"

"She has her lucid times, but they seem to be further and further apart lately. She does still recognize me, but she asked me the other day who the man was that I had with me. I could have cried. Dale and I have been married for nearly thirty years. I told Mom he was my husband, and she was upset because nobody had told her I was married."

Meredith reached across the desk and patted Lydia's hand. It was so hard to deal with this kind of situation. No wonder Lydia wanted to exonerate her great-grandfather while her mother could still be comforted by it.

"Anyway," Lydia said more cheerfully, "it really doesn't matter whether or not there's actually a letter. I want to find out about the theft, if it isn't too late."

Meredith got the pertinent information about Lydia's grandfather including his full name, his date of birth and date of death, the date of his conviction, and which prison he'd been sent to. Then she got more information about the family in general.

"What about the Van Ordens?" she asked finally. "Does the family still run the company?"

Lydia nodded. "There's only one left, as far as I've ever heard. Thomas Van Orden's daughter-in-law, Vanessa."

"Matt's widow?"

"No. I believe she was married to Thomas Van Orden's younger son, but I'm not sure what his name was. David, maybe?"

"I can look it up," Meredith said, thinking as she jotted down the information that the woman must be very old by this time. "I'll see if I can find out more about her too. Now, if you have it, I'd like to get the address where your great-grandfather lived while he worked for the Van Ordens."

"I'll have to look up the addresses," Lydia said. "There were two or three different places they lived during that time, according to my mother and grandmother. I'm sure I have something that would show the addresses. I'll get them to you."

"Thanks."

Meredith took down the other information along with the full names of Lydia's mother and father and her maternal grandparents. She also got Lydia's current address and the name and the address of the insurance office where she worked.

"What else can I tell you?" Lydia asked. "I don't know what kind of information you need."

"This will get us started. My partner and I can find out a lot from this much, and if we have questions, we'll give you a call. Oh, we also have a friend of ours who knows a lot about the history of Savannah. She's been very helpful in past cases. Is it all right if we talk to her about your case?"

"That would be wonderful. You're welcome to share this information with anyone you think can help."

"Great. Is there anything more we ought to know at this point?"

"I can't think of anything, but I'll keep looking for whatever letter Mom might be talking about. There's not all that much in her room. I don't know where it could be."

"It's possible, of course, that there never was a letter. Then again, sometimes people in your mother's condition hide things for safekeeping and then can't remember where those things are hidden. If you don't have any luck, maybe my partner and I could come by and have a look too. That is, if you think it wouldn't upset your mother."

"That would be a big help." Lydia stood up, looking relieved. "Thank you so much. I'll be praying that you'll be able to find something soon. I really want Mom to know for sure about her grandfather. This has weighed on her for so long."

Meredith stood too and opened the office door.

"We'll do our very best," she said as she led the woman out. "If anything comes up, if your mother remembers anything or if you think of something we could check out, let us know."

Lydia thanked her profusely as she went out the front door.

"*Pobrecita*. Poor thing." Carmen clicked her tongue sympathetically as she handed Meredith the messages that had come for her since she came in. "She was telling me about her mother while she was waiting."

"I know. I hope we can help her with this, but it's a very old case. Julia and I are going to have our work cut out for us."

Meredith heard the back door open and a moment later Julia came into the foyer, elegantly dressed and with every strand of her silver hair in place despite the heat.

"Sorry I'm running late. I must look a mess."

"Oh stop," Meredith said with a grin. "How's the car?"

"Mine or Beau's?"

"Either."

"Mine's in the shop. They have no idea what's wrong with it yet. Beau's is always hard for me to get used to, but it's fine. And he's okay with staying home for the day as long as he has Bunny to hang out with."

"That cat," Meredith said. "I don't know if you rescued her or if she took the two of you hostage."

Julia laughed. "I hope you both had a good Fourth."

"Harmony and I went to the beach," Carmen said. Harmony was the little girl Carmen mentored through the Boys and Girls Club.

"That sounds like fun," Julia said.

"Yeah, she's teaching me to swim."

"She is?" Meredith asked. "But you can already—"

Carmen gave her a knowing grin. "Sometimes it's easier to teach them if you let them think they have to help you."

"That's adorable. So true," Julia said and then looked at Meredith. "Looks like I missed our new client."

"Let's get some coffee," Meredith said, "and I'll tell you about it. Do you know anything about Van Orden Munitions?"

"Not much. I've seen a few things about them in the paper, about contracts with the government and that kind of thing. Why?"

"I was wondering about who owns it now."

"That would be Vanessa Van Orden," Julia told her.

"Really?"

Julia nodded. "Does she have something to do with this case?"

"I don't know, but I was wondering how hard it might be to get to talk to her."

"Might not be easy," Julia said as they walked into the hall to the coffeemaker.

"I was afraid of that. I was actually surprised to know that she was still alive, but I'd imagine she doesn't get out much anymore."

Julia frowned. "Why would you think that?"

"Maybe our client has her information wrong, but she told me Vanessa is the wife of Thomas Van Orden's younger son. He was running the company and had an older son go into the service in World War I. That was 1918. His daughter-in-law would have to be pushing a hundred at least."

"Well, I've seen her a couple of times," Julia said, following Meredith into her office with her coffee. "Either she has some great genes, or she found the fountain of youth. Vanessa Van Orden doesn't look a day over forty-five."